ACHILLE'S INTIMACY JOURNEY

Mario D. Rucci

First Edition (2020)

RUC BOOKS – Montreal, Canada

RUCCIAN BOOKS
(Books by Mario D. Rucci)

PARTICLES: World P Conception (WORLD BUILDING BLOCKS)
IDEOGRAPHS: World S Conception (WORLD BUILDING BLOCKS)
CONCEPTS: World M Conception (WORLD BUILDING BLOCKS)

WORLD CONCEPTION Chronological Version – VOLUME 1
WORLD CONCEPTION Chronological Version – VOLUME 2
WORLD CONCEPTION Chronological Version – VOLUME 3
WORLD CONCEPTION Chronological Version – VOLUME 4
WORLD CONCEPTION Chronological Version – VOLUME 5

TECHNOLOGICAL INVENTIONS

RUCCIAN ART VOL1

ACHILLE'S INTIMACY JOURNEY (Novel)

DEDICATION

To…

Mr. A. Cusano,
the greatest Fair Sex Tutor in the world

Miss N. Rinaldi,
the greatest Middle School Teacher in the world

Mrs. B. Preston,
the greatest College Mentor in the world

ACHILLE'S INTIMACY JOURNEY
by Mario D. Rucci

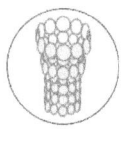 Published by:
RUC^{TM} BOOKS
Montreal, QC, Canada
Orders from RucBooks.com

ISBN, print ed.   978-1-989504-18-5
ISBN, electronic ed.   978-1-989504-19-2

First Printing 2019

TABLE OF CONTENTS

ABOUT THE AUTHOR

Mario D. Rucci is the 5th child of Nicola Rucci and Cristina Maria Del Russo. He was born in 1948 in Sepino, Campobasso, Italy. He moved to Canada with family in 1966, when he was 18 years old. He was a teacher for 30 years: taught fine arts in High School and all subjects in Elementary School. He retired from teaching in 2006, at the age of 58, to work full time on his writing. He worked on his writing for another 12 years, until 2018 (age 70). After that came the harder parts: correcting and editing.

Over the course of his life **Mario D. Rucci** has been a painter, writer, teacher, computer expert, house builder, inventor, theoretical physicist, and philosopher – and he has excelled in whatever he happened to tackle.

INTRODUCTION

Even though INTIMACY is somewhat autobiographical, it is a painting, not a photograph, of events. Inevitably, **events are painted by one's own beliefs.** And, we must not forget the first rule in creative writing: To make an event convey the overall narrative, some details have to be deleted, added, or bent in the right direction. So, in the end, these events are not factual events from the life of the author, but fictional events in the life of Achille, whose stories this work is about.

Each of these thirty-three stories is complete in itself; however, taken as a whole, they narrate **Achille's journey to establish intimacy with the fair sex**. In other words, it is about his coming of age with regard to his relationship with women. The conflict about Achille occurs when he fails to rise to the moment, due to the fact that he is immature, inexperienced, or insecure. Yet, despite these shortcomings, he obstinately pushes on towards the goal of his journey.

Achille's journey begins in Sepino, Italy, his birthplace, and continues in Montreal, Canada, where he settles at the age of fifteen. These events occurred during the time he was in school over a span of 3 **periods**: before High School, during High School, and after High School. Within these periods, the stories are organized according to **themes**, not according to a chronological order. For a clearer understanding of periods and themes, along with chapters titles, look at the table that follows!

ACHILLE'S INTIMACY JOURNEY

BEFORE HIGH SCHOOL
1. **Yearnings**: Annetta, Annina, Diana, Anna
2. **Infatuations**: Fioretta, Lucrezia, Ginevra
3. **Prospects**: Loredana, Angela, Sofia

DURING HIGH SCHOOL
4. **Contemplated Intimacies**: Concetta, Patrizia, Marianne, Jeanne, Stella
5. **Doomed Dates**: Francine, Maureen, Liane, Anne
6. **Romantic Pursuits**: Bianca, Louise, Amalia, Anita

AFTER HIGH SCHOOL
7. **Friends**: Jenny, Fanny, Eva, Vicky
8. **Lovers**: Debbie, Bree, Rosalinda
9. **Intendeds**: Monique, Ginette, Vita

ACHILLE'S WORDS FOR VAGINA
The Sepinese, a variation of Neapolitan, is Achille's mother tongue. Consequently, he prefers the Sepinese when he refers to the **vagina**. His Sepinese word for a young vagina, it is *patanella* (little potato); for an active vagina, it is *patana* (mature potato); and for a birthed vagina, it is *patanone* (big potato). This, of course, is his interpretation of the word. Not every Sepinese may think this way.

1A. My Yearning Annetta

MOONLIGHT VS. SUNLIGHT

I sit down at my desk
And I start to write.
The powers to recollect
are strengthened in me
in the intensity of night
under the moonlight.

But in the morning
the eye of light
stares at me.
I grow uneasy
and I scatter,
like the sunlight.

THE MAIURA FOUNTAIN DISTRICT

I grew up in a district just outside Sepino main cluster of houses. This district was located in the countryside, north of downtown, along the gravel road leading to Altilia, between two brooks. The south brook was blessed with Maiura Fountain and the north brook boasted a dam with a mill. This district was called the Maiura Fountain District because the people living in this area had to go to Maiura Fountain for drinking water.

I lived in the middle of a long row of attached two-story houses, home to my family with two families on one side and two others on the other. My family's house was the largest. It included 10 rooms, 5 on the ground floor and 5 on the second floor. But, it had no plumbing system, no cooking/heating system, and no indoor sanitation system. My mother had to fetch water daily from Maiura Fountain. For cooking and heating she had to use the fireplace. And, our toilet was the outhouse at the corner of the irrigation pond.

If standing in front of the house and facing the expanse of land in front of it, this is how the front yard looked like. On the right, there was a fenced artificial pond, used to irrigate the land, and an outhouse. On the left, there was a tall fence dividing our property and the neighbor's. In front, there was a well but the water was not potable. Scattered around, there were three or four plum trees, a peach tree, and an old olive tree. And, beyond that, the land faded out of sight as the ground lowered. The vineyard was at the very end.

It was this front yard that entertained my countless youthful activities, like playing with my dog Tribuline, swinging and climbing the plum trees, building a teepee, navigating a raft in the pond, playing soccer under the old olive tree, taking my first bike ride, pole-vaulting with my older brother, and catching fireflies at dusk.

YEARNING TO KNOW

The gravel road leading to Altilia ran behind my attached house. On the other side of the road, there was a detached house at right angle to ours. It belonged to Gianmarco's family. Gianmarco was my childhood playmate.

It was early summer, **the year before Gianmarco and I started going to school**. At the side of his house, where the land raised, two sturdy black-clothed women were working the field. Under the gigantic mulberry tree, in the cozy front yard, Gianmarco and I were sitting on the warm threshold stone. Gianmarco was rocking **Annetta**, his sister, a baby his mother had 'bought' a few months before.

The cradle went gently to and fro, the little girl slept, and the shadow of the mulberry tree fell on us and against the house.

"Have you seen it?" I asked.

"Yes!" Gianmarco said reluctantly.

"It's like a *patanella* (little potato), right?"

"Yes!"

I waited a while before saying, "Let me see it!"

"No. I can't. Mother and Grandmother will see us."

"They can't. See?" The two women in black had moved behind the corner of the house and gone out of view. "Come on, let me see it?" came my persuading, almost pleading, voice.

"No!" Gianmarco said in a firm voice. He seemed upset.

"Oh, you! Always the same! I'll catch you for this. You'll see!" I rose and started to go.

"Okay, Achille," he said. "I'll let you. But quick!"

He undid his sister's waddling. Just then **Annetta** woke up from her nap and looked at Gianmarco and the wide world around her. She kicked one of her tiny legs upwards. And there it was what everybody was talking about! But how ugly it looked!

"That's what it looks like!" I said.

"Okay, now?" said Gianmarco.

"Yes, Okay!" I said. How much meeker my voice sounded now!

Gianmarco covered up his little sister and I sat back on the stone threshold. Everything returned to normal, but my heart.

1B. My Yearning Annina

THE GAMES WE PLAY
We could play the game you like,
where you'd just snap your fingers
and I'd be at your beck and call,
like the puppy you've on a leash.

In the Maiura Fountain District, my other childhood playmate was **Annina**. She lived at the right end of the long row of attached houses.

One day, **when I was in elementary school**, Annina and I were in my kitchen downstairs. The small window was closed and covered to protect us from the flies and the heat of that summer day. We were talking in the cool of the semi-darkened room.

We'd just come from the vineyard, at the far end of the property, where my older brother Gianni had been playing some sort of mommy-and-daddy game with Annina. He would pretend of making love to her and she would pretend of giving birth to a baby. Annina used a small gourd for pretend baby.

The topic of the conversation had started with Gianni who had left because he had to do some errand for my mother. We were arguing about who had seen whose *patanella* in the hamlet.

"I've seen Za Giuannina's," I said. Za Giuannina was Gianmarco's mother.

"Me too," said Annina.

We were both lying, but it was a matter of prestige. Falling short of people to name, I said, "I saw your mother's too,"

"When? How, Achille?" said Annina.

"The day before yesterday. She was on the balcony. I was passing by."

I was triumphantly enjoying the advantage, when she said, "And I saw your mother's."

I was hurt. It was my mother! I wanted to argue with her, but then I realized that I had started it. After a while I said, "As to the biggest, there's none bigger than Za Maria's." Za Maria was our neighbor. The old woman had no children. When my mother worked in the field, she babysat my brother and me.

"Oh, yes," Annina agreed. "Za Maria's must be really big."

"It's like this." I said and I stretched my arms. That was silly. And we laughed. When I spoke again my voice was softer: "Do yon want to play with me, like you did with Gianni before?"

"Let's go!" said Annina.

1C. My Yearning Diana

HEED TO YOUR FACULTIES

Listen! it 's the tide against the reef;
I'm breathing your breath.

Touch! We're lying in a meadow;
my fingers are stroking your hair.

Hush! the crickets are chirping;
I'm unbuttoning your dress.

Feel! the air is fresh;
you're dropping your panties.

Halt! the moon is in your eyes;
I'm browsing on you.

Look! a thousand stars;
we're writhing ivy.

Behold! a star is falling;
we're whirling in space.

Hear! the night is quiet now;
it's time to go home.

It came a time when the girls in the Fontana Maiura District were growing up. Somehow, they were being told things that conflicted with what the boys were after. At first, they refused to play the mummy-and-daddy game and, later on, quit altogether playing with the boys. This change of things disturbed my older brother and me; because our eyes were set on **Diana**'s sweet forming figure. She became our most coveted prize in the district. Diana was Annina's older sister. She was my older brother's age. She had rosy cheeks. As she became older, she became prettier.

Diana was still in her early teens, when her mother, who had been a most active dancer in her youth, desirous to revive a bygone time and considering Diana had come to almost betrothal age, began giving dances at her house in order to expose her jewel and thus find her a suitor. Rarely a week went by that the district was spared of accordion music. Time went by. Diana was now in her mid teens and in bloom as attested by her rosier cheeks, but no suitable suitor had loomed at the dances.

A lot hinged on Diana's future. She was being watched over constantly, to my consternation and that of my older brother's. However noble the designs of the lady for her daughter, they interfered with ours. Then my older brother thought out a scheme. He told me that he would patiently wait in the communal outhouse, at the corner of the artificial pond, and when she'd go in, he'd grab her. I borrowed his idea and didn't tell him. I had many daydreams about grabbing her as she came into the outhouse and I was oblivious that my young imagination couldn't provide me with how to proceed after that.

At first, it seemed to me, that the little young lady either refrained from going to the bathroom or had a different timing from mine. It was only later, after many long waits in the outhouse, that I found out that, instead of the outhouse, she was using her barn, in all probability under the advisement of some wise guy in her family.

It appeared all was lost when one summer day, **when I was in elementary school**, Diana and I happened to be all alone in the Parche District, a far out uninhabited area in the countryside. We were watching her dozen sheep and my one goat in the pasture field that my mother was letting Diana's family use.

It was raining lightly, and so we both were repairing under my umbrella. At first we were both standing; but, later, we sat down on the fallow of a bordering strip of land. I had to get up twice. I wouldn't let her take turns to drive the sheep back where they were allowed to graze. Afterwards, the sheep and goat didn't move much and didn't bother Diana and me anymore.

Sitting on the fallow, under the umbrella, with the rain falling lightly, in that isolated place, a saught after yearning caught up with me. As I was sitting next to my young teenager, the cravings of so many schemes regarding her lighted persistently in my head.

"Since the sheep are calm, Achille," said Diana, "if you keep watch, I want to sleep for a while. I'm so sleepy!" And in saying that she yawned, tapping her mouth with her hand.

I said it was okay.

She crossed her arms on her knees and buried her head on the square of her arms.

The raindrops fell on the umbrella cloth producing rhythmic resting sounds, as if caressing it. A lone passerby, driving a donkey in front of him, passed by along the country road, behind us, at the far end of the field. He was going back home. The light rain had spoiled his rural work. I saw that he didn't notice us watching the sheep. Diana was still. The only thing that could be seen of her head was her long black hair. It seemed she'd shut herself off from the world around her.

I shifted the umbrella to my right   hand. I looked at the road, at the sheep, and at Diana. The place looked so immense, and yet it was so quiet. The only noises were the pricking of the rain on the umbrella cloth and the grazing of the sheep. The stillness that reigned around was an invitation to action. In that stillness, my hand moved. It crept on the fallow. It slid under the rim of Diana's skirt. As it moved forward, an inch or two at a time, my heart pounded without refrain in my chest.

The turmoil in my heart was somewhat eased with my progress. I advanced my hand, passing under Diana's right thigh, approaching the enticing goal. Under the skirt, in between her legs, I experienced a pleasing warmth, a most gratifying comfort. I constantly watched Diana's head buried in her arms and knees. I paused again, as to receive, from her being still, sureness to go on. All sorts of questions passed through my head. *Does she have any underwear? Won't she wake up when I touch her?* But these were just hindrances, blotting them out as they appeared. I refused to cave in to any of these deterring possibilities. I gulped down the ramifications of my trepidation and went on with my hand. Suddenly she stirred! I quickly pulled my hand out from under her skirt.

It was a false alarm, for she kept on dozing peacefully. Even though, more cautiously this time, my hand was again under her skirt, advancing slowly, barely touching the fallow. Water formed in my mouth. I'd been told that it was hairy. I'd never seen a full grown one. But my imagination and hearsay knowledge had worked wonders and the most beautiful of all had been pictured in my mind, with soft and fine hairs that touching it would make one squirm with delight. It only sufficed to go a little further. It was time to know. It was my chance to know. I arrived under her crotch. I pondered for a while and then began to lift my fingers from the fallow, slowly, the middle finger first, the others following. I touched what seemed to be the downy hair of her crotch, and then, for fear that she might wake up, I quickly brought my hand out from under her skirt.

I had touched it! And she didn't stir! I ventured my hand again for the third time on the same path that my fingers were learning by heart. As my hand travelled on the fallow with more ease, my mind tried to resolve the aftermath, once I came to touch her there. She was going to wake up. I imagined her waking up from sleep and looking at me with surprise. *I'll just shrug. No, I won't stop at that. I'll topple her over on the fallow. Take her by force if she resists. But, maybe I won't need to do that, as she'll let herself be caressed and make love to me.* My thoughts were dissipated by harsh reality, as I saw her move her head, and I quickly retrieved my hand from under her skirt.

Diana shifted for a while on her arms and then slowly raised her head. My face, colored and warm from my unquenched desire, could be read as a book. Luckily for me that Diana's sleepy eyes were still illiterate. She extended one arm out from under the umbrella.

"It stopped raining!" she said.

I removed the umbrella and placed it on the fallow. She was right. I hadn't noticed. "Yes, it did," I said.

"The sheep didn't bother you?" she said.

"No, they've been calm."

She was quiet for some time, as taking time to completely wake up. To me it seemed she sensed something about what I'd been trying to do. Maybe she too had wanted it to happen but I had taken too long. It was possible that she'd faked her being asleep all the while. All I expected now was a word from her. And I was surprised when she said, "Are we going to pick some cherries? We just get them and we eat them here. The sheep look as though they're not going to move."

"Okay!" I assented but that was not what I wanted to do. We would be just wasting time.

We rose from the fallow and, as we took our way to the cherry-tree, my mind was working again. *We go for cherries now and when we come back if she doesn't make her move, I will.*

We went over the little stonewall to get into the side narrow bushy path that brought to the cherry-tree and also to the country road. I thought I'd show my kindness to her when it came to the picking of the cherries, in the meantime. But, even here, things did not quite go the way I'd wanted. When we got to the cherry-tree, while I was still pondering on whether or not to climb the wet tree trunk, she'd already reached and got hold of a branch loaded with cherries.

We were breaking twigs from the branch to take them with us, when we heard the noise of overturned stones in the path. Someone with some large domestic animal had entered the path from the road. Diana told me to go and see what it was. I ran to the path leaving her behind still holding the tree branch. When I got to the path I saw that, out of all people, it was Diana's older brother, with their newly bought cow. I shouted back to Diana that it was Antonio. When she heard that it was her brother, she let go of the branch.

Antonio was surprised to find us there. We had left the sheep and goat unattended and, on top of that, we were stealing cherries. He only scolded his sister, who, as the older one, should have known better.

Then he told her to go home. Now that he was there with the cow, he would watch the sheep too. And that put an end to my fantasy!

Later, while sitting in the fallow and watching over the cow and the sheep and the goat while eating cherries, I was listening to Antonio's coaching voice on the art of lovemaking. He had taken it upon himself to instruct me about women.

"In the case of taming a woman," he was saying, "to make sure that she's going to be friendly to you, there's one certain way of going about it. You take her breasts in your hands and you fondle and caress them and you see how, in no time, she becomes, from a ferocious tiger, that she might be, to a mewing kitten. So sure this technique is that no woman can resist it. To be more precise it is an art. You have guaranteed results."

Eyes wide open, I munched on a mouthful of cherries, while in my mind I was yelling, *If I knew! If I knew!* I wasn't listening to Antonio's voice anymore, as my hands played, dexterously and progressively on Diana's burgeoning breasts. The expression on her face told me that she was yielding to my yearning.

1D. My Yearning Anna

PATANELLA
O lovely, spectacular organ!
I would give my right arm
To quench my nearsightedness
At the splendor of your secrecy.

UNDER THE STAIRS
I was in elementary school at the time. I was coming back home from an errand. When I crossed the front yards, out in the field, I saw Za Giuannina and some other women of the district, who were helping my mother with the wheat harvest. I heard children noises coming from inside my house. **Anna**, Za Giuannina's older daughter, was there. She was two years younger than me but well developed for her age. And there she was, running in the house on her long legs, playing hide-and-seek with Annetta, her younger sister, and two other children from the district.

My younger brother and my older brother were also there with Angelo. Angelo was a friend from the Colle District. I noticed the unusual cheerful mood of my brothers as they went about in the house.

I was eating when Angelo told me. They had been fooling around with Anna!

"You too?" I said,

"Yes!" said Angelo with a smirk.

My brothers and Angelo said that it was my turn now.

I went to Anna and told her that I wanted her to do with me what she had been doing with the others or I would tell her mother. As my younger brother and

Angelo played with the younger children, Anna and I went under the stairs, where they had been doing it before. I closed the door.

Anna spread the burlap sac on the cement floor. She undressed and lay nude on the sac. I knelt between her spread legs. Under the small light bulb, I gazed at it and I was amazed how beautiful her *patanella* looked. Fine short hairs had started to grow and adorned it. I remembered how ugly her sister's had looked to me when I was five years old. Her sister's had looked plumeless, whereas hers was getting ready to fly.

I was about to touch it, when I heard her crying. I had not given much attention to her whimpers as she was undressing. I now looked at her. Tears streamed down her face.

"What is it?" I asked.

"I... I... I am afraid. Mother might come and find us."

"Why, no. She won't. My brothers and Angelo are going to warn us."

She cried all the more.

I pondered for a moment, and then I said, "You don't want to do it?"

"No... I... I..."

"Okay! We won't then!"

"And you won't tell my mother?"

"No, I won't!"

She stopped crying immediately. She dressed up in all haste. She seemed too glad to go. I became remorseful I'd been considerate with her. Did she take advantage of my good heart?

When I came out from under the stairs, Angelo, seeing me so soon, said, "Well, Achille?"

"I didn't do anything. She started to cry and I couldn't."

"Ah, you!"

Nobody said anything to Za Giuannina at night when the women came home from the field; but Za Giuannina was a fox of intuition and Anna got her ration of slaps all the same.

THE OUTHOUSE

I sat in the outhouse, or rather, squatted on the seat. It was too dirty to sit on it. It was getting dark. Anna would be passing by in the front yards soon. She'd have to bring the sheep back in. As I was waiting and I thought of the times I had been with her in the corn patch and in the vineyard.

In the corn patch, I had such an erection that it was difficult to direct it down. Her long underwear, she'd pushed down to her ankles, didn't help. She jolted each time I touched her crotch with my penis.

In the vineyard, under the cover of the grapevines, she laid spread under me open-mouthed and distant. I wanted to kiss her the way I'd seen done in magazines and comic books, but my younger brother was standing there behind me waiting for his turn.

The noise of the sheep coming into the front yards broke my reverie. I peeked through an opening between the boards. It was her! I moved to the other side of the seat, stood there, and squinted through a bigger opening. I knew now that the sheep would come to a halt in front of the gate that she would have to open to let them in. This would take quite a while, as she would have to move slowly among the sheep to reach the gate and open it, and then come back and drive the sheep in and follow them inside. It was during that time that I was the most intent at my purpose. Anna moved among the sheep. When she arrived at the gate, I had reached climax.

THE RAFT

I was reading a comic book. I lay face down on the raft I had built myself. The raft was anchored at the edge of the artificial pond, right in front where Anna kept her sheep. When she came to get her sheep out for their afternoon grazing, Za Giuannina, her mother, was with her.

Anna saw me and exchanged some words with me. She was friendly. She leaned on the pond fence and stood above me, very close. She told me, proudly, that she'd made herself the mini skirt she was wearing. The mini skirt was very tight on her and the fabric was thin. I could see her inner thighs against the bright light of the day. Who could ask for more? The boards of the raft were hot. And Anna did not know of the hot desire she was kindling in me. I listened to her as in a dream and, pushing with my hands and sliding on the raft, but not too abruptly, shifted to a better position. I couldn't turn. My erection would have shown!

But nothing could fool that fox of Za Giuannina. When she came to the pond fence, she too exchanged some words with me. But she was unfriendly. She questioned my presence there and she told me that I should go and help my mother with some chore.

So, at the urging of her mother, off went my desired, ingenuous girl with her sheep.

THE BACK WINDOW

The place was quiet and deserted during the afternoon rest. I had this yearning in me. I came from the front yards and walked on the gravel road to see if

I could find Anna. The road was deserted. The black mulberry tree stood majestic and high in front of her house.

I remembered the day she was up on that mulberry tree, going from branch to branch trying to reach the first ripening mulberries. Gianmarco, her brother, my younger brother, and I were there, under the tree. She wore a loose skirt and I got a good view of her legs in all their glory. In the heat of the passion I felt, I told Gianmarco that I was going to get his sister 'one of these days'. Gianmarco didn't like that, of course. He went inside his house and who knows what he told his mother. The result was that Za Giuannina came storming outside, ordered her daughter to come down, hit her with her hand, called her some vulgar name, pushed her inside, and ordered her to do some house chore. And, since then, there was no 'one of these days' for me.

Kicking the gravel on the road to break the surrounding quiet, I decided to go and look behind her house. Nobody seemed to be there. And, then, I saw her! There she was, sitting under the cherry tree, with her knees up, with her skirt drawn back, and her legs uncovered.

As I saw her, I instinctively got out of sight, without the slightest noise, behind the corn patch. She'd not seen me coming! From behind the corn patch, I peeked. She seemed to be admiring her legs, focused on something on her thighs. If I went to her, she was going to cover up her legs. I paused for a moment and then, in a flash, I knew what I could do.

I retreated noiselessly, slowly at first and then hastily, back alongside the road and into the front yards. Considering where she was, I could certainly watch her from the back window of my house. She was directly underneath it on the other side of the road. I hurried across the front yards. I went inside, mounted to the second floor, went through two rooms, and got to the end room where the back window was.

Slowly I unlocked a wooden shutter. The lock creaked and so did the shutter. That window was rarely opened. Some of the panes were broken and a shutter was cracked in the middle. Kids passing by used the window as a target.

I opened the shutter just slightly. She was still there. She was staring at her thighs. Her legs were uncovered all the way to her crotch.

As I savored that sight, I reached for my penis. I hoped nobody would pass by and cause her to cover her legs. All the secrecy made the whole thing very exciting. I climaxed in no time. I looked again. She was still there, still in the same position.

I continued to use, every time I could, that back window. Anna and Za Giuannina had a lot of work to do behind their house that summer.

2A. My Infatuated Fioretta

AFTERWORLD
One day, this heart of mine,
whose fast pounding for you
hastened my dying,
will pound no more.
But the invisible hearts
of all those who really loved
will be the music pieces
of the interminable orchestra
which will play when we'll meet.
None of us will ever utter word;
there will be no need for words
for we can speak with our eyes

SEPINO
Sepino is located in Southern Italy in the hills of the
Appenines. It is easily distinguished from neighboring
towns by its highest structure, the wine-bottle-shaped
campanile of Saint Cristina Church. Saint Cristina is
the patron saint of the town.

What are **salient** about Sepino are its landmarks,
like the town square (*Piazza Nerazio Prisco*), the
Three Fountains (*Tre Fontane*), and the ruins of
Saepinum (*Altilia*). The town square is paved with
black bricks; it revolves around a huge circular stone
fountain; and, surrounding it are the town main
buildings, like the town hall, the post office, the church
of Saint Cristina, the nunnery, and the schools. The
Three Fountains is famous for its mineral water and,
from its perched location, one gets a bird's eye view
of the town. And, the ruins of Saepinum, currently
referred to as *Altilia*, in its heyday, used to be an

important trading post along the Roman sheep track (*tratturo*).

What are **more salient** about Sepino are its annual celebrations, like the making of the Christmas crèche, the pig custom or the end-of-the-year butchering of the pig, the New Year's *Bufù*, the Easter pastries, and the Saint Cristina's July celebration.

What are **most salient** about Sepino are its weekly events, like the soccer games at the sheep track, the promenades in the square, and hanging out with friends.

I discovered Sepino's downtown when I started going to school. I started school with grade one. Only a few downtown children went to kindergarten.

YEARNING TO BE LOVED

The kindergarten children used this room in the nunnery during the day. But, in the evening, it was used by the **first grade** boys, for their catechism. And I was one of those boys.

I was paying attention to what **Fioretta** was saying. But, I felt the immensity of the room around us, as we sat clustered in the center of it. I was taking it all in: the little statues of the Madonna, the big statue of St. Anthony, and the bouquets in front of them. I had smelled the flowers when I had entered the room. The window was partly shut, to reduce the noise from the square and yet keep the room fresh with the cool spring air.

Gianmarco and I had arrived late and we saw that the nuns were not there. It was a nun who had been giving catechism. However, this evening, some High School girls were there. These girls frequented the nunnery because they were thinking about becoming nuns themselves.

Because there were no more chairs, Fioretta took a small bench from a corner and placed it next to the rest of the boys sitting on the chairs. Gianmarco walked towards the bench and I followed behind him quietly.

To me, the girls were lovely, enchanting, and angelic. There were three of them. Their leader seemed to be Fioretta, the prettiest one. I focused on her as she recited the short prayer we had to learn by heart.

During a short break, I examined better the little statue of Christ on a small stool by the wall. The rectangular top of the stool was covered with white sharp pebbles, all of the same size. In the middle of them stood the figure of Christ with the crown of thorns and carrying the cross. I noticed that some pebbles were missing from His path.

I heard Fioretta whisper to the other girl, "Look what a little dear he is!"

"Yes," said the other girl, "I noticed. He's so cute!"

A third girl joined them. Fioretta talked to her. They pointed. "He's so quiet!" said the third girl.

At this point, an embarrassing uneasiness seized me. I was not supposed to listen to their whispers, but the bench on which Gianmarco and I were sitting was so near to them.

"They're talking about you," said Gianmarco to me.

"Quiet!" I said. I did not want to ruin the good impression the girls had of me.

Gianmarco was sitting in the middle and I was sitting at the edge of the small bench. Fioretta came to us. She made Gianmarco sit further out and she moved me further in on the bench. "There! " she said.

I just looked at her. My heart was racing. And she went back. Now it was Gianmarco who was sitting at the edge of the small bench!

THE SHARP PEBBLES

Catechism resumed. Fioretta began explaining the meaning of the little statue of Christ carrying the cross on the sharp pebbles. "You see this statuette of Jesus carrying the cross and His path covered with these sharp pebbles? The pebbles symbolize the struggle Jesus had to undergo to reach Mount Calvary where He was crucified. You all know how much He suffered for us, with the heavy cross on His shoulder. Now, in the spirit of Easter, you boys can make the way of Jesus less hard. The kindergarten children do this, but you can participate. For anyone of you who does a *fioretto*, a small sacrifice, we will take a little sharp stone from Jesus' path, so that His way will be easier. A *fioretto* may consist of a bouquet you bring, or five lire that you put in this box, or if you behave well during catechism."

"And," continued one of Fioretta's friends, "since it's almost time to go home, you can do a *fioretto* right now. You stay still and quiet for five minutes and we shall take one pebble from Jesus' path. All right? Good! Everybody quiet!"

Nobody stirred. One, two minutes passed. One boy began whispering to another next to him. What was he doing! He was risking that no sharp pebble would be taken from the path of Jesus! Then, to my relief, the boy quieted down. The five minutes passed with no other incidents. The *fioretto* was accomplished! One pebble was taken from Jesus' path to make His path smoother.

We were dismissed. This was the moment some of us had been waiting for in order to go into the town square and play.

I was about to go through the huge exit door with Gianmarco, when Fioretta said to me, "Wait a moment, Achille. We want to talk to you. Tell your friend to wait."

"Wait for me here," I said to Gianmarco,

I went back to the kindergarten room and stood in front of the girls. They were smiling at me. And, perhaps because of the attention they were giving me, I felt less shy. Fioretta began saying, "We are very pleased with the way you behaved. We like you very much."

"You have been very good."

"We have decided to give you a present."

"If you keep on being good, the way you have been tonight."

I was standing there in front of them, just nodding my head, overwhelmed by the attention they were giving me.

Later, as we were coming out of the building, Gianmarco asked, "What did they want? "

I sensed a streak of envy in Gianmarco's voice. "Oh, nothing," I said. I didn't want him to feel bad. I didn't tell him what the High School girls had told me. And I certainly couldn't tell him that they had taken a pebble from Jesus' path just for me.

"For you, Achille," they had said.

THE MAGNIFICENT TOWN SQUARE
We crossed the kindergarten's playground, came to the iron gates, and stepped onto the kindergarten

landing with its iron railing. There, below us, lay the magnificent town square!

The square, with its surrounding tall buildings and its center massive fountain, gave one the feeling of being in the huge courtyard of a castle. The square was now pulsating and teeming with life: cries, shrieks, giggles, shouts, and running noises. Almost all the children from the catechism classes had rushed into the square, and, with their games, had transformed it in a matter of seconds. The square was an enormous stage where everybody was an active participant, except for the few elders who happened to stroll in it, stiff and dull in the lethargy of their age.

But there were some boys who were going home right after catechism, like Gianmarco and me. We walked towards the church but did not go down the flood of steps that led from the Saint Cristina Church to the square.

"We'll wait here," I said to Gianmarco.

We had to wait for my older brother. He was three years older than us. And he was playing in the square.

All sorts of games were going on in the square: hide-and-seek, catch-and-rescue, guards-and-thieves, skipping rope, spinning top, and flipping a beer bottle cap through the maze chalked on the black bricks. But there were, of course, those who gave themselves to more enterprising play, and one of those was my brother. I was watching him and his like-minded friend. Both of them, 'armed' with saw-dust balls attached to an elastic band, were 'attacking' a group of girls. The girls shrieked but, in reality, they were happy to get the attention. And my brother and his playmate laughed!

I knew that all this exuberance in the square would not last long. Night was approaching. It was getting dark. Gianmarco and I were afraid to go home alone. We were especially afraid of walking along that short stretch of road that separated our countryside houses from the main cluster of houses that was the town center. Along that stretch of road there were no dwellings. That was why we were waiting for my older brother.

THE WATER PISTOL

The following evening Gianmarco and I were not late for catechism. When we got to the kindergarten room, Fioretta and her friends called me and took me aside to talk to me. Fioretta said, "Achille, since you were so good last night, and since we promised you a present, look at what we have bought you! It's a water pistol. But it's a secret between us. We are doing this only for you. Don't let anyone else see it."

"No, I won't. I'll put it here in the inside pocket of my jacket," I said.

I gave them the bouquet I had in my hand. It was for Jesus carrying the cross. And Fioretta took out for me another pebble from Jesus' path.

Later, sitting on a chair next to Gianmarco and pressing to my chest the water pistol in the inside pocket of my jacket, I listened to Fioretta and looked at the statuette of Jesus. And I thought of ways to get rid of all those pebbles in front of Him. Any *fioretto*, any little nice action, could rid Him of a pebble, according to Fioretta's words. And I thought and wondered whether or not the nice thoughts I had would count to rid Jesus of some pebbles. At times I had so many nice thoughts!

When we came out of catechism, with Gianmarco following me, I walked, through the playing boys, to the round, stone basin with its fountains at the center of the square. I took out the pistol, filled it with water under a fountain, aimed across the basin, and gently pulled the trigger. A thin jet of water came out of the plastic pistol and drew a momentary line in the water of the basin. I asked Gianmarco if he wanted to shoot. He said no. I loaded the water pistol again, and this time I pointed it towards the square, where I was not going to wet anyone. The jet of water came out of the pistol and went far, and retreating drew a darker strip on the black bricks that paved the square. The last drops in the pistol fell at arms length from my feet.

At that moment, my older brother arrived and said, "What is it? Who gave it to you?"

I told him.

"Let's see," he said. And before I had time to reply he took it from me. He loaded it and in a sudden quick movement he aimed at his playmate. The latter tried to avoid the jet of water and ran away.

"Gianni!" I shouted. "Give it back!"

Later that night, all three of us were headed home. We were walking through the Colle District. The light of the day had given way to the shadows of the night. I held my pistol with all my force. I wasn't going to let my brother take it away from me again. For me, the pistol was precious because it was a symbol of the love Fioretta had for me. For my brother, it was just a toy.

BANG! BANG!

The day after, at home, I was sitting on the steps of the inside staircase. It was before catechism. There was still time.

I rested my chin in my left hand, the plastic pistol in the other, and I remembered last summer when I was playing with the other boys of the neighborhood in the threshing area with the wheat sheaves stacks all around us. I saw in my mind's eye their actions as they moved stealthily, creeping, squatting, or hiding among and in between the narrow corridors of the stacks. Slowly, as the recollection became clearer in my thoughts, my playmate's words became one with mine: "Bang! Bang! I shot you! I shot you! No, you didn't. I win! I win! You don't know how to play. You couldn't see me. I was behind this stack of sheaves. But I see you now. Bang! Bang!"

My older came in from outside and distracted me from my reverie. He sat beside me on the step.

"Will you lend me your pistol?" he said in a cajoling voice. "If you lend me your pistol just for tonight, I'll let you have any two pictures you like in my old history book. You always said you liked it."

"Yeah, but you're going to break my pistol," I said.

"No, I won't. I'll be careful."

I thought about it for a moment and then I said, "Show me the book again."

He rose and went into the kitchen. In a minute he was back with the book. He gave it to me and sat down next to me. As I looked through the pages he said again, "You can choose any two pictures you like."

I remembered the night before when I had thought that my older brother might enjoy the pistol better than I did. Pointing at two paintings by Leonardo, I said, "Okay. I'll take these two."

YOU'RE DEAD!

That evening I arrived late for catechism. I was still home when the catechism bell rang. My older brother had left a long time before me and Gianmarco was not coming. When I entered the kindergarten yard, I was panting and sweating from the long run from my house to the center of town. The kindergarten door was closed. I made myself more presentable by combing my hair with my fingers before reaching up for the doorknob.

I was expecting to see some nun, but instead one of Fioretta's friends opened the door. I said good evening but I did not get much of a response. As I entered I saw that all the boys were right inside the door. Most of the boys were sitting on the steps that led up to the corridor. I stood by the wall. I was still sweating. I wiped the sweat off my forehead and with the same gesture I set my hair. And soon I found myself repeating with the other boys the words of the prayer they were learning. The girls were standing with their backs to the door. There were just two of them tonight, Fioretta and the one who opened the door for me.

During a pause, I heard Fioretta say to the other girl, "Did you tell him?"

"No, I didn't. Not yet," said the other.

I sensed they were talking about me. And the confirmation came when Fioretta's friend approached me and said, "Achille, at the end of catechism stay behind. We want to talk to you."

At the end of catechism, when all the boys had gone out, Fioretta's friend came up to me and said, "We are very disappointed in you. We were mistaken about you."

I looked at her, incredulous. I did not know what she meant. "What is it?" I asked.

"Did you give the pistol to your brother or did he take it away from you?"

"I gave it to him," I said. "Why? What happened?"

"Your brother and that other scoundrel he's always with got us wet. We were at the kindergarten landing when he came up the church steps and sprayed us with water."

"And," continued Fioretta, "we don't like it much being sprayed at by our own water pistol, the pistol we bought. Have your brother give it back to you!"

"I will," I said, mortified by what they were telling me.

"Once you get it back," continued to say Fioretta's friend. "We want you to give it back to us. You have disappointed us, and we have all the right to claim our gift back."

As I was leaving, I was walking in front. Fioretta and her friend were coming after me to lock the gate. The front yard was wet. It had rained a little. The world around me seemed more desolate than the empty front yard. This was all because of my brother. He had ruined the enchantment!

I became aware of the noise from the square, as we came to the iron gate. The square was alive with the thundering noise made by the children. In all that ruckus, a noise right in front of me caught my attention. On the landing, outside the iron gate, a bunch of shrieking girls were trying to get away from something. I followed the source of their distress and I saw my brother. He had come up the church steps and was spraying at the girls with my water pistol.

"Gianni! " I shouted and ran after him by sliding under the railing and jumping on the church steps.

Among the shrieks of the girls and the noise coming from the square, he did not hear me.

"Gianni! " I shouted again after my brother, who, his deed done, was running away now with his inseparable playmate. I ran after him down the steps, but he was faster than me and I had to slow down if I did not want to trip and fall. When I reached the base of the steps, I stepped into a puddle of water gathered by the rain. The water splashed up and wetted my face. I stopped and stood there. It was because of all the anger that possessed me that I did not cry.

THE FUNERAL

That night, going home, in an even greater darkness than usual, I was crying. I carried the pistol like a dead bird in my hands. Between sobs I found enough breath to whine at my brother, "What have you done? How could you? And you even broke the pistol! The spout is bent here. And it doesn't shoot water anymore!"

"Don't make up stories," my brother was saying. "It's nothing, I tell you."

"Nothing! You say it's nothing," I said, this giving me a chance to vent my despair and misery even more. "After what you've done? It's all your fault!"

And then I remembered that Fioretta had seen me go under the railing and run and shout after my brother. At the thought that I had let her see me that I was just like all the other boys, I felt even more miserable and I sobbed all the more.

RESTORING UNIFORMITY

The following evening, in the large kindergarten room, before the start of catechism, I gave the pistol to

Fioretta. I told her that it was broken and then added, "I'll buy you a new one."

"It doesn't matter, " she said and, on examining the broken pistol, she added, "We'll keep this one." There wasn't much warmth in her voice, though she seemed more sympathetic than the others. All the favoritism she had shown me the first two nights was gone.

"Even so, I want to buy you a new one." I said

A few moments later catechism began. Fioretta and her friends were talking but I was not hearing them. They seemed to be talking only to Gianmarco and the other boys! I was anxiously waiting for the moment they would dismiss us.

There was a certain resentment between us. But in some way I was relieved. Now that they had seen that I was just like the other boys, I could be myself, not what they wanted me to be.

Because it was Easter, the crosses in the large room had been veiled with fine velvet cloth. Devastated as I was, I noticed something. All the pebbles had been put back in Jesus' path! What had been the use of the *fioretti*, then? I asked myself. But now I could see what had been missing before. With all the pebbles back in the path, the whole arrangement of Jesus and the pebbled path was a more pleasing picture. Yes, the picture was better to look at this way!

2B. My Infatuation Lucrezia

MY SECRET CRUSH
The first time I saw **Lucrezia** I was **in grade three**, during the summer, in downtown Sepino. My older brother and I were going for private tutoring to Mr. T's house. She was there with her older sister for the same reason. She was in grade two. She was delicate, beautiful, and shy. I showed off to her my drawing skills. After tutoring, I convinced my brother to go their way to find out where they lived. It didn't take much convincing my brother because he was interested in the older sister.

The second time I saw her it was later **that same year** in school. In class, Gianmarco and I sat in the last desk because we were taller. My friend turned towards me and said, "The second grade girls have no teacher today and some of them are coming to our class." Lucrezia was one of them! And, during the time she was there, I took every opportunity I had to glance at her.

I was in middle school at the time. One evening I had just reached the town square when I saw Gianluca, a schoolmate of mine. He was drawing on a stone of the sidewalk with a pencil. When he saw me, he said, "Ah, here's Achille! He's going to draw it for me." And then I noticed my secret crush standing there and impatiently waiting for her pencil. I did the drawing that he wanted me to do. When I finished, I noticed that my secret crush was flushed and uneasy. It was a good thing the she did not hear my heart pound uncontrollably and see that my uneasiness was greater than hers. She got her pencil back and went away in a hurry. I thought about that event for a very long time.

From then on, I longed to see her. I looked for her every morning before school. My heart would thump, thud, and pump faster every time I met her. Once I came face to face with her on the steps of the Castelli District. She was going in the opposite direction. And, another time, watching a fireworks display from the square with a large crowd of town folks, I planned to stand not to far from her. And, once, under the colorful explosions in the sky, our eyes met. O my poor heart!

During all of middle school, my longing for her never faltered. Once she had a small part in a play at Saint Stefano's. And, another time, she became a member of the Sepinese folklorist group. I have no doubt she got those parts because she was so beautiful. I cherished my thoughts about her. I daydreamed daily about her. And, I dedicated a little diary to her.

A PLUM EVENT

A most marvelous event happened that summer day she came to my house with her aunt and her cousin. Imagine my surprise when I saw her walk into our front yard. I was under the plum trees in my tiny, self-made swimsuit. She glanced towards me as she followed her aunt into the house. I rushed upstairs to get dressed. I put my hand on my chest to steady my heart. Then, from the window I saw her picking some plums. Alas, they were not ripe yet. My father told her in his usual rough way.

They didn't stay long. But, I'll always regret I didn't go and talk to her and show her my parents' estate. I wrote a poem about her visit and her plum tree.

THE PLUM TREE

The tree, which you craved,
O you who did not love me,
Whose plums you plucked
With your delicate hands,
(And my father's gruff voice
That wanted your desire stop.)

Lies dead in the front yard
By the merciless water,
the cause of that fate,
Stronger than the tree,
Mirror of its suffering
And of its bold figure.

Your historic coming
Was to me bittersweet,
Was to me bitter anguish
to my loved country estate,
It made me love a dead tree
That was dear to you, my Lucrè.

Next day I got up quite early. It was marvelous to see the pink-colored sky where the sun came into view. I had never experienced the dawn this way. It made me feel part of the surrounding nature.

The chilly dawn air reached my bones. I did not mind wetting the end of my trousers as I walked in the wet dew of the meadow. But I feared that I might step on the tail of some poisonous snake. I was there to pick a pear. The taste was sweet and juicy. And, throughout all that, I daydreamed of my Lucrezia.

When I got back, a harsh voice hit me. "What are you doing? Do you want to get sick?" My father, from the second floor bedroom window, was yelling at me.

FROM CRUSH TO LOVE

She had the loveliest body. She had delicate, refined forms. She had perfect proportions. Her whole figure was so symmetrically modeled that you'd soon realize that was a masterpiece of God.

My longing for her was so much different from the ones I had had for other girls. Case in point, one day I was standing by the stone basin in the square. She was bicycling in the square around the fountain. As she passed by in front of me, I could see much of the inside of her lovely legs. I could see the brown spots made by the bike on the inner sides of the thighs. But I didn't get aroused.

I regarded her with a lack of baseness. But I just had this feeling to possess what was so unattainable to me. This was the kind of girl I would have married on the spot, if I could. Every night, before falling asleep, the same prayer went out of my chest, "O Madonna, let it be that Lucrezia be my wife one day!"

I remember one night I went to the outhouse among the stones of a broken pigpen. I was afraid and I looked around me at the shadows of the fig tree, the plum tree, the vines, the basket willow, and the olive tree. And then I looked up at the giant vault of bright stars watching over me. I was in awe at the power of God and I prayed. 'O God, help me. Let Lucrezia be mine one day.'

Days and weeks and months went by, my love for her becoming day by day stronger. And I hadn't even for once talked to her! Hopes that lay outstretched far ahead. "O Madonna, intercede for me to our Lord. I promise I will not do this unhealthy thing I'm doing, so that this be the pledge of my vow, and you let Lucrezia be my girl one day."

AFTER YEARS OF LONGING

Suddenly, Lucrezia and her family moved to Campobasso because of her father's work. Still, they would spend their summers in Sepino. Then, one summer, I was stunned when I saw a boy from out of town with her. His name was Gianni. Giancarlo, a mutual friend, told me that he had seen them kissing behind the big rock along the Three Fountains Road. Later, I witnessed myself their passion during the Saint Cristina Dance in the square when I saw them in each other's arms dancing. Their fire was too great. It dashed all my hopes I had harbored all those years.

I couldn't dream about my Lucrezia the way I used to. It took me falling in love many times over with other girls for her to slowly fade from my mind. Even now, when I think about her, I grow sad.

2C. My Infatuation Ginevra

THE GRIM REAPER SPEAKS
When a leaf falls
from the living branch
to the dead ground,
you'll be coming to me.
This time it's me who runs the show.
And you'll do what I tell you to do.

Ginevra was the younger daughter of my parents'
friends, zi Giuanne and za Vittoria. They were also my
oldest brother's godparents. They lived downtown in
the Colle District.

THE SNOWSTORM
Every year, in Sepino, countryside families held the
pig custom. A family would stock up for the winter with
pork by killing a pig around Christmas time. The
family would invite relatives and friends to help with
the task and a big meal would follow to celebrate the
occasion.

This event went through three stages. The first
stage was about restraining and bleeding the pig. The
blood was gathered in a large bowl and used to make
blood sausages. The second stage was about
scorching and scraping the pig's skin with a curved
knife over on impromptu outdoor fire. And, the third
stage was about hanging the pig from the ceiling and
cutting the different parts.

The pig custom that's most vivid in my mind is
from the year there was an unexpected snowstorm. **I
was in elementary school at the time.** All the

guests, relatives and close friends, at my house, couldn't go back home. The feasting had been finished for some time. They'd been waiting over many bottles of wine, but the snowstorm didn't give any signs of stopping. It was late at night. It was decided they would stay over for the whole night. In the meantime they would help my mother with the sausage making.

My mother took all of us children to bed upstairs. The children included Ginevra and her older sister, my cousins, my older brother, and me. The bedroom was above the kitchen. The girls were to sleep in one bed and the boys in the other. In our bed, my older brother and my cousin Angelo were at the head of the bed, and my cousin Raffaele and me at the foot of the bed. My mother arranged it that way to have all of us fit in the large bed and we all had our own pillow. The bed sheets were icy but I was too excited to mind. My mother turned off the light and left.

In the darkness, I was thinking about Ginevra in the bed next to mine. Just later, I was about to fall asleep when someone turned on the light in the room. I was zi Giuanne, standing by the doorway. He was checking on his daughters, Ginevra and her older sister.

TATIGLIE'S PASSING

Ginevra was a little bit younger than me. She had a picture-perfect face with curly, short hair and dreamy, black eyes.

It was at the end of summer, **the year I finished middle school**, in the front yard, when zi Giuanne came near the well where I was cheerfully talking to Ginevra, his daughter.

"Uaglió! Don't you see your grandfather's dead?" he said with tears his ayes. And he started praising the dead's worthy merits.

This was the second time in the day an appeal was made to make me cry for the death of *tatiglie* (grandfather).

The first time happened in the morning when I was having breakfast in the kitchen and Za Maria had come from upstairs to tell me that my grandfather had just passed away. I put my spoon down and the old woman told me a second time, a tone of supplication in her voice, as she burst into tears.

At night, visitors were assembled for the wake in the dead's room upstairs. In the kitchen downstairs, right under the dead's room, Michele, my cousin, with his transporting power of telling stories, made all of us, my brothers and me, laugh heartily and loudly. He was telling us about his riding a stubborn donkey that bought him someplace else instead of where he was supposed to go. We quickly realized our folly and went upstairs to join the other mourners.

THE VISIT

The eve we were to leave for Canada, Ginevra and her parents came to pay a visit. That evening I was playing soccer in the front yard when they arrived. I went to change and comb my sweat-soaked hair upstairs. I showed them my sketchbook.

"You draw some beautiful legs," she said. I couldn't help glancing at her legs.

"'Uaglió! What is that bulge?" said zi Giuanne in an anxious voice and pointing at my Adam's apple. "It's big!"

"No, it's not big," she said. Then, referring to the drawings in my sketchbook, she said, "I would frame those."

"You don't want him to give you one, do you?" said her mother.

Later on, when my mother and her parents were talking about marriage, Ginevra turned towards me and to get my attention, she said, "Hey!"

"What is it?" I said.

"Nothing," she said.

When they got up to leave, I shook hands with her twice. I promised I would send her postcards from Montreal.

3A. My Prospect Loredana

SHE NEVER KNEW
It was that body that haunted,
that appealed, that enticed.
Oh! the lust she awoke in me!
and she never knew, never knew!

THE STAIRWAY
The last year in middle school was a watershed year for me. I excelled in all subjects, even when it required standing in front of the class and answering questions from the teacher. That year they had decided to separate us by gender. But, we did share the coat hangers outside the classrooms with the girls.

One day, after school, on the way home inside the Castelli District, my best friend Ezio told me that **Loredana** had boasted with her girlfriends that she liked me. His girlfriend had told him. Most of my friends had girlfriends.

"Listen, Ezio," I said. "I am the one who asks the girl, not the other way around."

We had come to the street door of his house. We said goodbye. Left alone, I started to take long strides down the long stairway. Lower down the stairway, whom do I see but Loredana with two other girls! She lived in the Colle District. Without slowing down, I said, "Hi!"

"Hi!" said Loredana.

As I continued at my quick stride, I heard them giggling behind me.

THE CONFESSIONAL

When I crossed the nave of the church, I knelt and bowed my head toward the altar. The Bravo boys, waiting for their turn at the confessional, were laughing. The fools didn't know that was the way you had to genuflect during the Passion Week.

Through the round, little holes of the grating I was able to locate Don Mario's face, as he moved slightly his head. I was in such an awe of Don Mario! We kids used to play soccer with him. But now, in the confessional, this young priest had transformed himself. He was no longer friendly. He was there to judge you!

Don Mario's voice came steady and firm from behind the grating, "Achille! Have you been doing one of those unhealthy things?"

"Yes!" came my half-choked voice, as I grappled for my answer. My heart was beating fast.

"To yourself?"

"Yes!"

"Do you do it often?"

"Yes!"

"See, Achille, you shouldn't indulge in it, because it becomes a habit, it enslaves your body." He paused for a moment and them added, "Try not to do it again, eh, Achille?"

"Yes, I promise."

"That's good, Achille! Is there anything else you want to tell me?"

THE BALCONY

All the church bells of the town let free to a joyous ringing. The sound, with all its eloquence, reached and filled the Maiura Fountain District. It was Easter

Sunday! I had just come from downtown where I'd been taking my mandatory yearly communion.

My mother and brothers hadn't come home yet. I was in the kitchen upstairs, where my mother used to bake the Easter pastries in the wood-fired oven. After I ate my favorite Easter pastry, I went out on the balcony. From up on the balcony, at the end of the long row of houses, between Zi Ntonie's willows, where the gravel road bent, I could see the town folks, all flaunting their Sunday best, going back to their country homes.

It was sunny, a beautiful, bright spring day. Trees were in bloom. I looked down at the fine display by the plum trees around the large irrigation pond. In the summer I would be climbing their trunks and have a bellyful of plums.

The earth seemed to emanate so much more energy. Plants, animals and people went about their calling with renewed vigor.

I looked again towards the gravel road. Loredana was passing by with Michele's sister! She was going to her grandmother's house.

Inadvertently, I touched with my crotch the bars of the balcony railing. The railing was warm. I felt a strong yearning. It was a long time I had not masturbated.

I went inside and sat and stretched my legs. It did not take long before I was melting in pleasure. It was all Loredana's fault!

Then I recited a Confiteor and asked God's forgiveness. I'd resisted such a short time! Sighing, I renewed my promise, the promise I'd made to Don Mario.

3B. My Prospect Angela

CHANCE OCCURRENCE
Angela is a discovery made
because I once knew Rita
and Rita because I knew
other Ritas before her.

THE FEAST
It was a town holiday, a feast. The main asphalt road was flanked with stalls of every sort on both sides from the Colle District to the square. These were stalls by out-of-town dealers and peddlers who had swarmed into Sepino from all over the surrounding towns with the prospect of making money. The animal fair, as usual, had been held in the Colle District throughout the morning and the afternoon. The small circus and the merry-go-round had been installed there too. The square and the Uascere were full of stalls too; cards and roulettes and other similar games; the ice cream truck at the corner of the Uascere; but mainly target and shooting stalls, with prizes to win; the balloons attached to the string going up high. What a sensation it was to use an air rifle for the first time! "Come and shoot! Ten shots for fifty lire! Show us what a fine soldier you are!"

I was in middle school at the time. I was standing by the railing of the Uascere with my countryside friend Fino. I'd never really been able to fully feel at ease at a feast. I was more of an observer than a participant. But I liked the fact that it was here that, among the throngs of people, I was likely to see Lucrezia. She took a new wonderful look in her holiday clothes in the so many lights and sounds of the square or in the Uascere or the stretch of asphalt road before coming into the square. She would be promenading with her girlfriends, licking an ice cream, listening earnestly to the noise, or gazing with lost longing eyes to the crowd of people.

Fino and I strolled close to the railing behind the target-stalls. Below, at the bottom of the wall, tons of shoe marquees could be seen.

"Doctor Vespa told Carluccio that, if he doesn't stop masturbating, he's going to die," said Fino.

"Yeah!" I said, "Carluccio, with his skinny constitution!"

"It must be dangerous in some way. Doesn't it, the sperm, come from the brain?"

"I don't know!" I said.

"I tried to stop, but I couldn't do it for more than five days, a week at the most."

"I think I've found the solution," I said proudly. "It's four weeks now since I last masturbated. For the first time in my life I have wet dreams."

"How did you do it?" he said.

"I made some sort of vow. Till now it has worked."

I felt proud of myself. I'd been able to resist that long! The vow was since Lucrezia's visit to my house. I'd finally made up my mind. All the other previous times I had not kept my word, but this time I did. It was thanks to her.

THE GIRL

The two girls were sitting on the bench. Fino and I stopped by the railing directly in front of them.

"Buy us an ice cream, Achille!" said **Angela**, the daughter of Zi Francische. The other girl sitting beside her was the girl from the Cunvente District, the girl who sat with Pierina in class.

"I can't," I said. "I don't have any money." But I lied. Anyway, all I had was two hundred lire. And I knew that poor Fino didn't have any money.

If we'd bought them an ice cream, we could've asked the girls to go for a walk with us along the road to the Tre Fontane, a mile of winding road from the town center, a wonderful place for lovers because it was scantly lighted. We could've come to kiss them there, but my love for Lucrezia stopped me. The image of Lucrezia, whom I had seen just before when I was walking about with Fino, was so much alive in my mind!

THE WOMAN

Late that night, after Fino had left to go home, I approached a stall, not too far from the bench. The stall was made of three-foot-high wooden panels forming a circle. A small tall table stood at the center of the circle. The table was covered with liquor bottles of different shapes. If the player would catch a liquor bottle with a plastic ring, he would win it. The stall belonged to the couple that owned the target stall at the other end of the Uascere. Husband and wife would take turns at the 'catch-a-bottle-with-a-ring' stall. Now it was the wife's turn.

Men, young and married, crowded around the stall when she was there. That didn't happen with her husband. The woman gathered the plastic rings and handed them, three at a time, to the players. Then, from time to time, holding three rings high up in her right hand and wearing a bunch of them like a bracelet on her left forearm, she shouted, "Three for fifty lire. Come on, gentlemen. Try your luck and win a bottle!"

She wore a sleeveless, close-fitting, one-piece summer dress that struggled to restrain her bounteous breasts. She was ever sensual in her movements. She bend down to pick up a plastic ring, raised her arms high up in the air, and whirled around so that everyone could view her from the front, the side, and the back. And, the more views I got of her, the more I wanted.

When I was back home and in bed late that night, I daydreamed of being with and kissing Angela along the road of the Three Fountains. She'd called me by my name! Then the image of the woman at the stall came calling with a more enticing voice. I was assailed by the fullness and maturity of her sensuality. My arm stretched down under the bed covers. In no time, I was released by pleasure. The vow I had made thanks to Lucrezia was in tatters.

3C. My Prospect Sofia

A SIMPLE TOUCH
I felt, when I touched her arm,
the resistance of her muscles,
the roundness of her form,
the warmth of her flesh.

FIRST TIME
I was in middle school at the time. The first encounter with **Sofia** was at Michele's house. Michele, two years younger, and his brother, my age, were my playmates in the countryside. Michele, his sister Francesca, Sofia, and I were the only ones at the house. Sofia was Michele's age and Francesca was two years younger.

At first, we went for walnuts. I was paying a lot of attention to Sofia. "Ah, you're here just for Sofia?" said Michele. I wanted to leave but she convinced me to stay.

Later, we were lying on the bed. I had my arm around Sofia's shoulders.

"What about Francesca? You are not hugging her," she said.

"Sure I am. Can't you see?" I put my other arm around Francesca, to make her happy.

There was a knocking on the door downstairs. Michele suspected it was his father. He jumped from the window. I went downstairs to open the door. Zi Pippine had to suspect there was something wrong because we had locked ourselves inside. Michele came from outside and his father swung a slap at him. "Idiot, what are you doing?" he said.

Later on I went home. Sofia came with me. We were going in the same direction. She lived downtown.

"Let your older sister Rita come down, tomorrow." I said.

"Why her? I am here," she said. She was jealous.

SECOND TIME

The second encounter with Sofia was at harvest time that same year. She was baby-sitting my neighbor's newborn. My neighbor was in the field helping my mother with the wheat harvest.

As usual I got up late. I had just washed my face. She came. The day before I had been all day with her and in the evening I had escorted her home. She started to tease me. I was in the right mood. I took her in my arms and said, "It's easy, you see. I'll teach you. Open your mouth." And I bent forward to kiss her on her lips. She sprang up and hit my upper lip with her teeth. Then she ran away. I stayed there in front of the mirror massaging my lip.

In the afternoon, she sat for me and I marveled at her beautiful legs. She seemed to care for me. In the evening I played a puzzle game with her. She had to guess the first letter from each of the pictures I had drawn. The letters spelled 'SOFIA BELLA'. In the evening, I escorted her home, like the night before.

THIRD TIME

Then I didn't see her for a long time. When I saw her again, a year later, I was coming from playing soccer at the sheep track. I was with my friend Marco. We met her on the New Road, just before the cemetery. She was going in the opposite direction with her sister and her sister's boyfriend. Marco flirted with her. She giggled to his jokes. She paid no attention to me. And I did the same.

LAST TIME

The last time I saw her was a couple of days before my leave for Canada. She had come with her older sister and her mother to my neighbor's house. I was putting my shorts on upstairs in my bedroom. I heard them coming to my house. I leaned out of the window and found her looking up at me. I promptly retreated inside. They didn't stay long and went back to my neighbor's house.

Later, I was playing soccer with my younger brother and my neighbor Gianmarco in the front yard. She came near the fence and said, "Gianmarco, can I come over there?"

"Don't ask me. Ask Achille," said Gianmarco.

She didn't dare ask me. What was the use? In a couple of days I was leaving for Canada. I didn't deem her to be a likely romantic prospect in my life.

"Play, Gianmarco," I said.

4A. My Contemplated Intimacy Concetta

ART, MY WIFE

Cry, cry out, art,
You, that of life,
Are a true wife,
A pulsing heart.

You feed on joy
And depression.
My ambition
Is your fond toy.

Yet, you do give
A moment's heed,
My bitter need,
That makes me live.

MONTREAL

Montreal is located on an island in the St. Lawrence River in the province of Quebec. Montreal is a multicultural city. French is the official language of Quebec. Two thirds of the people can speak English. And Italian is the third most spoken language. Montreal is a global commercial center with all the perks it offers weighed against the pollution, congestion, and tension that come with it.

In my new town, I went from mild to extreme with regard to weather, population, and potential. The weather in Sepino was mild and temperate, whereas in Montreal the weather went from very cold in the winter to very hot in the summer. In Sepino, with about two thousand people, I knew everyone either directly or indirectly; in Montreal, with about two million people, I was restricted to the few people I met in the neighbourhood, at school, and at work.

One thing seemed to be a carryover, however. In Sepino I had to contend with standard Italian taught in school against Sepinese, my mother tongue. In Montreal the struggle was between English, my choice, and French, the official language of Quebec. The large Italian community in Montreal learned English in school and used French at work. However, because of the confusion of bilingualism, Italians also retained the language of their country of origin.

OUR NEW ACCOMODATIONS

After we arrived and after all the visits from relatives and friends during the weekend, I spent the Monday afternoon writing letters for my mother to relatives and friends in Italy. The bulk of the news consisted in describing the apartment and in listing all the amenities, like the oil-fired heating, the electric range, the refrigerator, and the plumbing system (our own indoor 'fountain', the bathroom, and the bathtub). I appreciated the amenities a lot, but the one who was the most excited about them was my mother, because that meant no more gathering sticks to light a fire, no more fetching drinking water, and no more hand washing in frigid water.

In the letters to my friends I talked about the house comforts, even though in a more vague and general way. I related to them the experience of the airplane flight. I told them how one could buy a car starting from $ 250.00. (I had seen this in an Italian tabloid.) And I also wrote to them that on TV one could watch a movie avery day, not just twice a week.

GIRLS GALORE

We were in the car, my oldest brother, my younger brother, and I. My oldest brother was driving. We were in the downtown area. I could see in the near distance or right above me the tall buildings and skyscrapers my friend Angelo had told me about. We came to a street whose sidewalks were crowded with people. A policeman in the middle of the street signaled my brother to drive on.

"We can't stop here," said my oldest brother.

My younger brother and I did not know what was going on, why all those people were there. My oldest brother knew but he would not tell us. It was some kind of surprise. So, having parked his car further down, we followed our big, hasty brother. All the three of us were running to get back to the street where the crowd was. It was around the end of November; the air was colder; winter was approaching.

We stood with the people who were waiting for something. There were so many people! They were dressed in their plaid shirts and winter coats. Some parents had hoisted their warmly dressed children on their shoulders.

My oldest brother declared, "It didn't pass by yet."

And, then, the Santa Claus Parade on Sherbrooke Street arrived. The first thing that I saw left me thunderstruck. It was an image that stayed imprinted in my mind forever. A squadron of young girls came marching up at the sound of drums and the cadenced noise of their feet. And they stopped not far from us! They repeated the excise, swinging their batons and flags at the direction of their conductor. They were all wearing the same colorful jackets, the daring mini-skirts, and the embroidered cowboy-like boots. Oh, a wall of legs, a squadron of legs, hundreds of legs!

They gave me the same feeling that I once had about a swarm of butterflies I had watched in the wheat field. They were within reach but they could not be caught. My oldest brother made a remark but I could not be bothered by what he was saying. The heart pounding, I was trying to see which pair of legs was the prettiest!

That night in bed, before falling sleep, I daydreamed about that squadron of girls in their mini skirts. Then, I imagined the blond girl wearing the elephant pants, which I had seen when playing soccer in the street during the day, marching in front of the parading girls. And she was the prettiest! I realized that, instead of my Lucrezia, I was daydreaming of her. I was constructing English sentences to say to her when I would go out with her. At the end of the movie I would say, "How did you like the movie?"

I remembered again Angelo's words: "There, it'll be like being born again: a new language, new friends, new surroundings. I already see you, under those skyscrapers, looking up and getting a sore neck to see their tops." Yes, a new life. Of this, of all these things I was certain. But, my greatest yearning was that, in this new country, I too could have a girl of my own. She would be a Canadian girl. I would love her. And I would embrace the land to which she belonged!

Once again, Angelo's words came to me, "There, it'll be like being born again." His massage was clear. My Italian Middle Ages had ended, and my Canadian Renaissance was beginning.

MISSED MARRIAGE
When we came from Sepino, her parents were among those who came to visit. That evening,

Concetta sat in the living room and watched TV with my brothers and me. She was about my age. I exchanged very few words with her. I did learn that she had stopped going to school to go to work.

There was some talk between her parents and mine about her and me getting married, but I would have none of it.

Later, she married this guy I knew. He came from the same countryside district as her parents. Once, in Sepino, my mother and I went to his house and he played marbles with me.

The only other time I met Concetta was about **five years later**. I was coming from school. I was walking fast on the sidewalk. I didn't know it was she but I recognized her husband, his lanky figure. She walked in front of him with their firstborn who was pushing the empty baby carriage. He came behind her, holding the last born in his arms.

"Hello!" I said to him.

"Why, it's… Achille! Hi!"

A reciprocal, fast, rushed "How are you? He extended and opened the hand he was holding the baby with. I shook hands. There was a momentary pause.

"How are things, Pasquale?" I said.

"Oh, taking a stroll with the wife and kids."

So, that was she! I nodded towards the pretty baby clad in late autumn clothes. The baby remained reserved and distant as she was. Her husband was speaking standard Italian to me instead of Sepinese.

"You're coming from school? Your brother Vittorio, is he here?"

The skin of his upper lip sticking to the teeth as he opened his mouth! Yes, it was he, a memory resurfacing, that evening we'd played marbles together.

"My brother is in the States," I said in Sepinese.

"And your mother, how is she?"

"She's all right," I said. "What can you do? Old age."

There was a pause. I looked sideways, at her and at the firstborn.

"Everything okay?" I said.

"Yes. Everything's fine," her husband said and looked at his possessions, his wife and sons. "Me and my family."

I smiled and straightened the cap of the baby he was holding. "You have a beautiful family," I said.

"Thank you," he said. "Well, see you, Achille!"

"Bye!" I said to him and then to her, "Bye!"

She started pushing the empty baby carriage and didn't answer. I did not say hello to her at the beginning; so, she did say goodbye to me at the end.

As I was crossing the incoming street, I thought that the reason why she did not say goodbye to me was either because she did not approved of my long hair and beard or because she was a woman scorned. It was very likely the latter reason.

4B. My Contemplated Intimacy Patrizia

BEAUTY
O Beauty, how can I long for death,
When you invigorate me with health?
I am not afraid of mortal knives,
When my realization of you arrives.

Patrizia's family immigrated to Canada around the same time as ours. In Sepino, she and I had been schoolmates. In Montreal, we became friends, and I tried, different times, to have a romantic relationship with her, but it was not meant to be. My story with her centers around 3 conversations I had with her.

THIS PIG LIFE!
I was doing **my last year of high school**. It was in the middle of winter. I talked to Patrizia on the phone. She said that she wasn't very happy. "This pig life!" she said. And she talked about suicide. I felt very much for her to the point of crying and to the point of taking her in my arms and covering her with kisses.

I'LL PHONE YOU!
A month later, I called her up.
   "I was going to call you up," she said.
   I told her about the summer courses at Dawson, something she'd asked me to look into. And, as we often did, our conversation turned to talking about Sepino.
   I invited her to go out with me. Right at that moment the phone line went dead. I called her back.

"I can't talk now," she said. "Are you home tomorrow? I'll phone you, okay?"

Three days later I was still waiting.

I'M GETTING MARRIED!

A year and a half later, I met Patrizia at the Sauve Metro Sation, by the Fleury bus stop. And we had the following conversation.

What's new? [What she said is in *italic* font.]

Not much. [What I said is in regular font.]

Aren't you going to school?

Yes. College.

I'm getting married in three weeks!

You're getting married. Ouch, you're fast.

Oh, well. It's something that happens to every girl.

And to every guy!

Oh, yes.

Are you happy?

I guess I am happy. Oh, yes! I am happy!

That's good.

I want to go back to school after I get married; but I don't know if I'll have the time.

One thing is for sure. You're going to have kids.

Kids? Oh, come on, now! (Tapping me on the shoulder.) No, I won't, for at least three years. To have children at my age! What do you think, eh? I'm not going to ruin my life.

You're right. I know a guy who just got married and they decided not to have children for a while. I think everybody does this nowadays, especially if you marry at a young age.

Yes. I don't want to.

Is the boy you're getting married to Italian?

No, he's Arminian.

I asked because every Italian girl usually seems to get married to an Italian boy.

No. Why should he be Italian? Once you find the boy you like…

Yes, you're right. It's not a must.

And what's new with you, Achille?

Everybody seems to get older than me, not in age, I mean, but in progress, as I look at the people of my generation. You, for example, two years younger than me, are getting married. My old school friends…

Yes, but guys get married at an older age. When you find the girl of your dreams, even you…

It's not so much finding the girl of your dreams. I think it's a matter of what you want to do in life. For the moment, I want to study.

What is it you want to be?

A teacher and, during the long summer breaks, I intend to write. So, you're getting married!... Do you remember when you came to pose for me?

Yes. I still have that drawing… I've changed now, haven't I?

Yes, and very much so. I told you, last time we met, remember?

Yes, you told me. But I don't want to change too much. I don't want to look old, you know.

Ah, you're not old. You just look more serious. Perhaps because of what's happening to you. You're getting married! I wish you to be very happy!

Thanks! And good luck to you, Achille!

Thanks, Patrizia!

4C. My Contemplated Intimacy
Marianne

ENIGMATIC MARI
That girl, there, with my dear friends,
Surely *Italiana* as her rosy cheeks!
On the stairs I sit sideways to her.
As she speaks, talks to her friend,
I become aware of her white teeth,
The cherry-colored flesh of her lips.

O those eyes! the clear white!
The plucking of her eyebrows!
The flicker of light in her pupils!
Lovely she is, my enigmatic Mari,
But she goes out of sight,
fast gone but unforgotten.

I was in high school at the time. I went to the Manpower Center. It was 11:45 when the lady at the reception desk told me that Mr. Gagnon had told her that I had to come back at 1:00. I then went, as I had planned, to the Unemployment Office on Clark Street, to see if something could be done about the termination of my claim. No, there was nothing they could do for me. The Welfare Benefit seemed to be the final solution, but I didn't want that.

I had time to loaf around, so I went down St. Lawrence Blvd. again. In an attempt to kill time I thought of going to Gianmarco's factory, on Port Royal, even with no hope of my being put to work there. All at once, a mass of people came out of the two main large factory buildings and who knows where else from. While I made my way amongst the people, women and girls mostly, it was to my surprise and joy to see Maurizio just come out of the second, new building.

He told me that, after he had quit his factory job, they had called him back and, on top of that, met his demands. After I told him why I was there, he said that he was going to meet Laura, his Intended, who was working on Chabannel Street, not far from there, to have lunch with her. I went along with him. After waiting for a while, she finally came out, and with her was a girl, a very pretty brunette.

After saying "Hello!" to Laura, the two betrothed pondered on where to go to have lunch. Laura suggested to go on the stairs inside and then told her work companion in French, "*Sur l'éscalier.*" I followed them.

Inside, on the staircase, they settled on the middle landing between the ground floor and the basement. Laura soliloquized on her forgetfulness and spoke of introductions. I thought she was talking about Maurizio too, but she meant only me. She waited on the steps for me and introduced the girl to me. **Marianne** was her name.

"*Piacere!*" she said a little ahead of Laura's end of the introductions.

"*Piacere,*" I answered, realizing that she was Italian Canadian and not French Canadian. (In deference to Maurizio, we were speaking Italian; even though, the rest of us would have been much more comfortable speaking English.)

They sat on the top step of the last flight of stairs. Without thinking I quickly sat on the landing. They had their back to me.

"*Mah, le spalle!*" protested Marianne.

"*Non fa niente,*" I said.

"*Almeno là*," said Laura pointing.

And I went to sit on the bottom step of the above flight of stairs, so I would face them from the side.

Marianne rose to go to the restaurant to buy something to drink. Meanwhile Maurizio passed me some grapes and I took them but I refused any other food, saying that at one o'clock, after having been at the Manpower Center, I would be going home.

Marianne returned from the restaurant and, noticing I wasn't eating, she said, "*E non volete niente, voi?*"

"*No, grazie,*" I said; and I explained that I was going home.

Later, because Marianne was blocking the traffic on the staircase by sitting next to Laura and Maurizio, she sat lower down in front of them. This way she was facing me.

To entertain us, Maurizio proclaimed that the factory called him back because he was 'good stuff'.

Laura protested his mock conceit.

Laura said to Marianne that I was '*un vecchio amico*' and I continued by saying that Maurizio and I had worked together and we used to talk of her. Marianne was looking up at me with those big wonderful black eyes. I naturally often stole a secret glance of her to feast on those beautiful legs barely covered by her dark-blue mini skirt. Those very legs I had fancied about when coming inside and going up the stairs. And I remember that my eyes rested on the secret enticement of the back of her knees.

I got the impression that, when I looked her way, I met her look of approbation. And this was what puzzled me. What could she find in me? Anyway, I arranged my legs to a more pleasing composition from her point of view. I was going to put my best foot forward, even though I could not know about her romantic intentions towards me. One could never tell. But who more than I wished her romantic intentions to come true!

I played with the residue of my finished grapes against the railing. Marianne trashed a peeled orange on which she had just given a bite. Was it shyness for eating in front of other people, that nasty sensation which had often attacked me in the past? Oh, Marianne!

Then I went to the restaurant to get some matches for Maurizio. When I came back, he offered me a cigarette.

I thanked him and said, "*E le* 'ladies'?"

Maurizio repeated my gaffe. I had combined Italian and English.

Laura answered with wit, "*Le* ladies don't smoke. *Le* ladies smoke smog only."

To recover from my blunder, I asked her what she meant, but it was impossible to salvage my shame. That gaffe weighed on my head for the rest of the time I was with them!

Maurizio said he felt tired now. Laura suggested a walk outside, and so did Marianne.

"*Se si cammina un po', si digerisce pure,*" I said.

So we went outside. Marianne took care of the trash, under Maurizio's encouragement. I remember I held the door for them all when we came to the ground lobby.

We walked towards St. Lawrence Blvd. The girls were in the middle. Marianne was on my side. But the sidewalk was too narrow for the four of us. I was the one who would separate from the group when pedestrians and trees came our way.

Laura and Maurizio talked about school. Maurizio asked Marianne if she'd passed and she said, after a suppressed laugh, "Sotto al ponte." I gathered that

Laura and Marianne had gone to the same school. I wanted to ask about their schooling but I didn't. In fact, I said nothing all the way to the end of our walk. More than ever now I felt I was playing second fiddle to the group.

At the corner of St. Lawrence Blvd. when there was finally more than enough room to walk comfortably together, Maurizio and Laura were preparing to part. It was 12:45.

"Come on," I said to Maurizio to induce him to kiss Laura as I had on the stairs. But he didn't.

I sought Marianne's attention to say goodbye to her.

"Bye!" she said. And was there regret in that goodbye?

I then went into the building with Maurizio. I thought of asking him about getting Marianne's phone number through Laura, but then I decided I'd better not. We parted. It was 12:55. He went back to work and I went to take the elevator to get to the Manpower Center floor.

When I was waiting for Mr. Gagnon, the thought of Marianne came to my mind, incessant and distressing, as I reflected on what had happened. I rebelled against my romantic intentions. I knew I couldn't, I shouldn't. There was a realization that I was going to hurt myself. It was happening all over again. I could not allow it to happen, even though it was ecstasy to linger on the thought and the hope of possessing that girl. Was it finally possible that, just for a change, a girl would be in love with me? But vain were my protests!

The thought of her assailed me again at home. There was so little on which my happiness could thrive. I had to contend with there being no money and my going to school for the next five years. Yet, how wonderful it would be if I would get that job Mr. Gagnon sent me to! It was right behind the building she was working in. I would have the chance to daily meet her with Maurizio and Laura! How wonderful, my God, it would have been!

Whatever good impression I had made with Marianne at the beginning, I squandered it with my language gaffe and my reticence to engage. But, it was mainly my self-deprecation that prevented me from achieving any sort of success with her.

4D. My Contemplated Intimacy Jeanne

FLIGHTS OF FANCY
She comes, sits slowly, demurely,
puts her hands between her knees.
I go, kneel at her bare feet,
I stroke those naked arms,
holding those soft breasts
in the palms of my hands,
under the flimsy garment,
promising to nurse my lust.
Now, my lips are going to join
with that sweet budding flesh.

I was in high school at the time. It was a Monday in July. I went for a job interview and took the wrong bus. I was sitting in the back and I watched this toothless guy, with his 'contracted' English and his habitual Canadian 'eh!' at the end of each sentence, talking to these two guys. One, who wore glasses, looked like Angelo, my friend from Sepino. And the other one, with his wild hair, looked like a visitor from the red planet.

A petite girl came and sat on the seat in front of me. She was plump, curvaceous, and abundant in form. Soon after, her girlfriend joined her. My plump girl was utterly pretty. She had black hair, long eyelashes, and spectacular lips. Her round face was the 'ice cream type', the type you would lick. When she and her friend got up to get off the bus, the realization came to me that she was short in contrast to my long body. I was getting off at the same bus stop. I was pleased so I could keep looking at her and delight my eyes. My enjoyment was of short duration.

She was going to the clothing store with her companion. I had to gratify myself by giving a last glance at her and follow the couple of middle-aged people going to the bus stop across the street.

As I was standing at the bus stop, a young girl crossed the street and the marked delineation of her crotch was an appealing sight to see. I thought she was coming to stand at the bus stop too, but she went the other way. I wasn't at all cross as I turned my attention to a young girl in short I had seen, just a moment before, coming my way. She was now in front of the clothing store with another young girl, a skinny companion of about the same age. The legs of this girl in shorts had appealed to me from far and my body craved in the expectation of having her nearer me. She seemed to reciprocate my look of discovery and for what happened later I now know she did.

She came with her friend and stood at the bus stop. I exchanged a glance with her as she was approaching and the sweetness of it may hardly be told. The look a got was so fresh and young as the young thing who emanated it. I could see a filling in her full sensual mouth. I could also notice now that her shorts were fluffy around the large round thighs. She was standing at my left. I knew now she was French-speaking by the language used by her friend, who spoke to her nonstop. She seemed shy of the hoarse talking of her friend and it seemed she wished her friend would quiet down. I exchanged more glances with her and she gave me to understand that I met with her approval as she did with me. Her friend stopped talking and went and sat down on the stones bordering the sidewalk and invited her to follow, but 'my girl' said no and stayed beside me and drew near, ever nearer, almost touching me, just a hair was there separating us. That she was petite it did not matter.

She looked good at my side. She gave me the feeling she was mine. She threw behind her shoulder-length hair. She was there, near me. I had my arms crossed. I exchanged another glance with her. She was shy. So near! I wanted to say, "Give me your phone number!" My mind shot to the future when she was already mine and I was caressing her body. Her breasts were not highly developed, but they were young and blossoming.

She rendered me slightly uneasy. Her young age, her schoolgirl looks, and her bashfulness could not but excite in me an inside lust which would not and could not show outwardly. I forced myself to look here and there pretending to be attracted by this and that; but, what I wanted to look and stare at in interminable time was at my side, drawn near, and slightly moving.

A woman with a very young girl came at the bus stop and I watched with tenderness that growing frail thing. And then looking behind I saw an old middle-aged woman with her shopping bags, sitting beside my girl's girlfriend.

Even my girl was trying to be natural and looking somewhere and nowhere. But I had decided to continue to look at her and, whenever possible, in the most natural way, I did. In one glance I saw her respond passionately to my look of want. To be mine! I saw desire in her eager eyes, in her mouth, in her face, in her whole body. I was aroused by her desire, her youth, her closeness. God, what am I doing? The desire I had for this young body increased with each successive sweet glance that demanded fulfilment. She eyed me from head to toe and in such an expressive and manifest way, as to hide nothing of her intentions.

I once moved closer to the couple in front of me, to see if I was right, and she followed me and stood as close to me as before. I knew now. But what was I going to do? I had to act, but I did not know how. It seemed as though our bus was coming and it was now that I grew again uneasy. My heart grew wilder and precipitated in hurried heartbeats, because I didn't want to get on the bus. I wanted to linger with my girl of desire.

Time seemed to pass slowly until the bus came. I was determined to get first on the bus as to have her follow me to my seat. But the bus stopped before the stop sign and she was getting on the bus first. I made things worse by lingering behind to let the couple get on before me. I saw her turn, look behind, and look at me; as for fear I was not going to follow her on the bus. It was her friend who paid her fare. I was getting on; she was sitting right in front on the side seat. She moved to one side of the occupied seat as to make room for me. It was too tight! I sat on a single seat in the middle of the bus across from her. She continued to cast more glances towards my direction. And I was practically looking at her all the time. It was the woman with the shopping bags who broke this enchantment. She began conversing with her, retaining her attention. I fancied she was acquainting her on the art of love, warning her about me, or merely teasing her on young love. But my girl was still, when she could, casting glances at me.

Was she going to get off when I was? At the St. Lawrence stop most people got off. There was more room; there were more seats. She invited her friend to sit by her. The latter got up and made her notice they had to get off, to my puzzling expectation. And my hope! Was it perhaps my turn to get off too? No, it was only Tolhurst. I had three more stops to go yet. I fought with the decision of getting off with her; but, then, what could I do? Wouldn't that have looked like I was following her? Adieu, my girl of desire!

And then the soothing thought that, after I finished with my job interview, I was going to return to where she got off and look for the one who was also looking for me.

I did do that but to no avail. I failed because I did not engage with her.

(I thought that her name might be **Jeanne**, because St. Jean is the patron saint of Quebec.)

4E. My Contemplated Intimacy Stella

AUTUMN
It is autumn in Canada. The leaves are dead!
Leaves, on the streets of the city of Montreal,
Are stirred by a breeze or blown by a gust.
And that autumnal air purifies the lungs.

Are they dead leaves or are they living ones?
Are they alive on the sidewalk and dead on the tree?
Is the green leaf on the sidewalk still alive?
Or, is it the brown leaf that is still on the branch?

Perhaps, it's a question of old and not of life.
They were young at their birth.
Then, they have come to their end,
Unconscious of how much we owe them.

Autumn is the most beautiful season.
And it is these leaves that make it so.
A leaf that I picked waves in my hand
And in all the corners of a large country.

Autumn is a season to gawk at and enjoy,
Until the cold of winter enters in our bones
And this too we'll learn to love and cherish,
Because Canada is a country that owns.

WINTER
It happens in the winter **after I finish high school**.
Stella reminds me so much of the woman at that
Saint Cristina's feast.

At work, near the yarn weavers, I tell her, "I want
to ask you something, but don't be offended. You

know all the respect I have for you and I always will, whether you accept or you don't accept what I want to propose to you. I'll always respect you. But I need to tell you, whatever your answer will be. I hope that you won't be upset for what I want to ask you... I have often dreamed of you, especially lately. I have thought how beautiful it would be to make love to you, to have you for me, to be able to caress and be able to show how much I love you, how much love I have for you..."

"Achille!" she darts back from me. But I can see that, though surprised by what I am asking, she is pleased.

Ah, to caress her, as that night when I met her on the bus with her daughter! "Your face is all wet!" I said and, with affection, I ventured to wipe out the melting snowflakes from her face with my hand and my gesture turned into a caress.

I want to bring her to a hotel where I thought of bringing her daughter. She finally accepts my offer one day out of an emotional breakdown.

On the bed I undress her. We lie down naked. We kiss on the mouth. She has me in her hand. I have her *patanone* (big potato) in my hand. She massages me, building me up for what is to come.

"Oh, Stella! My Stelluccia!" I moan.

My fingers are in the tangled secret hairs of hers. I'm sucking now her tongue, now her lips, and now her cheeks. Her face is wet with my saliva.

She stands up. I'm looking up, between her legs. She slowly comes down to sit on my crotch and bends forward for a hug.

Her legs squeeze against mine, her breasts flatten against mine, and her mouth presses against mine.

Stuck together like that, we rub against each other until we come both at the same time with shakes of pleasure in a shatter and burst of a thousand little white stars, a sweetness which is not from sugar, a pain which is not from a wound, and mingled together in a spasm of indefinable deliverance.

"Oh, how sweet you are, Stella! You're sweet and good, my beautiful Stelluccia! Beautiful, beautiful Stelluccia!"

And we make love two more times because I need it and she needs it.

SPRING

Three months later, we are lying on the bed, in that same hotel. Her beautiful tummy is protruding. I fondle her tummy; I lie with my ear on it; and I kiss it. She says to me that she has to go to that clinic. I want the baby, but there is no choice. She also says we have to stop seeing each other. It's more dangerous now.

"Can't we still see each other, anyhow?" I say.

"No!" she says.

I cry. She cries.

"I don't want to lose you," I say.

"You won't lose me," she says.

"You say that to console me," I say.

I know I'm not going to be making love to her again, to this woman bearing the fruits of our love.

One night, at work, I hear her in the women's toilet. She is crying in there. I go in and stay with her even though she wants me to get out. I can see her protests are fighting her desire for me to stay. I hold my older woman in my arms. She is someone else's mother, someone else's wife, and **my contemplated lover.**

5A. My Doomed Date Francine

MONTREAL METRO
She walked down the platform,
escaping far off to the other end.
Following behind, going to her,
would have looked suspicious.
Later, a large crowd gathered,
rendering her flight more complete.

TO THE LIBRARY
I was in high school at the time. I was going to the public library. The drunk on the Sauvé bus slid his lower lip against his upper one and stuck it out. With his lower lip protruding like that, his profile took the appearance of a Leonardesque caricature.

When I got out of the Sherbrooke Station and went to take the bus, a young girl was walking in front of me. She wore green pants patterned with red riders on white horses. The bus arrived. Everybody ran, including my fancy dressed girl. I took it easy and I got on the bus last.

On the bus, I observed the girl's long hair parting at the top of her head, descending down, and reaching her buttocks. She turned to chat with her girlfriend's boyfriend who hung her blond hair with his hand to show its length. He gaped and she giggled. Her behavior was uninhibited and warm. When she laughed, her lips parted in so graceful a way to exhibit the even, splendid row of her upper teeth. How wonderful it would have been to make love to her!

I bathed in the natural beauty of this girl who didn't have a tinge of makeup on her face. Once, she met my stare and I was overcome by its ecstasy, but I had to turn away to make it seem it was a casual glance. I hoped she would get off when I was getting off, but she didn't. Anyway, I was thankful to live in Montreal where beauties like this ravishing girl existed.

FROM THE LIBRARY
I was coming from the public library. In the subway, on the platform, I watched two girls passing by and I thought of Liane on Mount Royal and that blasted panty hose. Alongside the shallow artificial lake (*Lac des castors*), as we were looking for Francois (my friend) and Claudette (her sister), I had my hand inside her pantyhose and stroked in slapping motion her buttocks.

When we got on the train, a city employee stood by the door and cornered me at the end of the subway car where I was sitting. He prevented me from people watching. I strongly wished that he sat down.

Nevertheless, I spotted this couple. I thought they were Italian but then I heard them speaking French. They were about thirty years old and overweight. They glued to each other, especially the woman, with one hand of hers in his coat and one hand of his in her trench. The next moment I looked at them, they were kissing. He had his hand in her lap and it seemed he was fondling her round belly and reaching for her prominent crotch. I could already imagine him prodding and prodding at her. The woman was a little shorter than the man, but both were short and barrel-like. That they belonged together it was very explicit.

I turned my attention to the girl standing by the opposite doors. Her slender body, her rippling undulating hair coming down below her shoulders, and her thin waist... I imagined her recognizing me and coming to me to talk to me about a book I had written about subway passengers. "I didn't know that a nice girl like you would be interested in my work!"

She turned towards the doors. That put an end to my reverie. She was getting ready to get off at the next stop. I saw that the wing-like corners of her mouth had curled up into a magical, delicious smile. She was perhaps smiling on account of the fat couple. I was smiling too. I don't know exactly why. Was it also due to the fat couple? Perhaps. But things were so perfect in that moment that I found myself smiling in elated contentment. I zeroed in on her countenance as she turned to glance at me. I was received by that tender smile of hers. I was smiling with her in an uncontrived and unplanned reaction to her smile. But I had to look away immediately, not being able to withstand the beauty I had found in our complicity. I was afraid that such a wonderful moment might end badly for me because of the apathy I might have found in a more aware, second look of hers. When she got off I watched her, stately striding out of view.

Then, this girl got on. She wore white shoes, bluish grey jeans, a red sweater, and a black coat (of the same material as her jeans) that matched her parted and tied-back black hair. She stood erect at the center pole in front of me. You could tell she stood on her toes. Her stance was erect and aligned, her heels and knees touching, her neck and head upright, and her bosom pointing at right angle to her body. She stood there straighter and more graceful than the pole. As if guessing my observing thought, she bent a leg, her unbuttoned coat widened a little more and she partly showed the tender angle of her crotch. Before I was curiously interested in her, but now I was definitely in love with her. And I was aroused! At the Sauvé station I thought she was getting off with me, but I was wrong. I woke up from my trance just on time. I squeezed between two male passengers and stepped off the train just as the doors closed behind me.

FROM THE LIBRARY AGAIN

This other time I was coming from the public library, in the subway, I noticed this girl. She got off at the Sauvé Station like me. We both took the Fleury bus. She sat somewhere in the middle and I sat in the back. She was glancing at me all the time. When she got off, just before my stop, I got off with her. I caught up with her.

"Excuse me, Miss. Do you speak English?" I said.

"*Non*," she said in French.

"*Je parle le Francais, un peu; mais, je ne sais pas comment dire...*" I started to say in French.

I, I understand English," she said.

"Oh, that's better."

"I speak English but I don't like to speak English. I make a lot of mistakes."

"Oh, I see. I'll be brief," I said.

"Brief?"

"Brief. Short. I'll try to be short with what I want to say. Here it is. I am attracted to you. I would like to give you my phone number. Then, if you like, you could call me. And, we could get to know each other."

"Huh?"

"Will you phone me, if I give you my phone number?"

"Okay," she said.

"Just a minute now and I give you my phone number." I stopped walking to write my phone number on a piece of paper. Then, I ran to catch up with her. "Here it is. Will you phone me?"

"Okay."

"Do you want me to accompany you?" At that, she shrugged her shoulders. "Do you live around here?" I asked.

"Yes, I live on Foret."

"I don't know where that is."

"And where do you live?" she asked.

"I live near the Fleury Hospital. Do you know where it is?"

"Yes, I know."

"Well, will you call me?" I said.

She giggled a little. "If I phone you, I don't know your name."

"Oh, you're right. My name is Achille."

"Achille?" She pronounced the French way.

"Yes, Achille. And what is your name?"

"**Francine**. Look!" She showed me her purse. The name FRANCINE was etched on her purse.

"It's a pretty name. Do you work?"

"Yes, on St. Catherine."

"It's a little far from here. Is your work interesting?"

"Yeah. I sew pockets."

"I see. It's a factory."

"Yes, a factory."

"I also worked in a factory last summer. So, I know how it is like."

"What do you do? Do you work?"

"No. I am still going to school."

"Where?"

"I go to Pius X. It is at the corner of Papineau and Sauve."

"Yes. I know." She stopped in front of a block apartment.

"Oh, this is where you live?"

"She nodded.

"Will you call me?"

"When?"

"Oh, I don't know. This weekend. Whenever you want. Okay?"

"Okay."

"Bye, Francine!"

"Bye!" she said.

I never heard from her again. This time I did engage with the girl, but I made the very big mistake of giving her my phone number instead of getting hers.

5B. My Doomed Date Maureen

In the middle of winter, **when I was in high school**, I went to my Typewriting Class in the evening.

When she came in, she looked around. She had the choice, but she sat next to me, in the back. She was ever so sweet! She was lavish with her attention to me. And she was such a mouthwatering morsel with that alluring ass!

Looking for a mate? I'm here!
Come to me. I'm aroused!

The cold seat I was sitting on brought me to my senses.
  "My name is **Maureen**!" she said.
  "How do you do? My name is Achille!"

Amid the cacophony made by the typewriters, every once in a while, she'd nudge me and say, "*Bene?*"
  I'd answer, "*Benissimo!*"

Adorable reverie, promise me panacea.
But, careful, cougar! I'm a pussy.

"You're sure you don't mind giving me a lift? I said.
  "You're so sweet!" she said.
  "You're very sweet too!" I said.
  "You mean that we can already tell that we like each other?" she said.
  Yes! Yes! Yes!

She looked so happy as we walked on the noisy pebbles of the parking lot to get to her car. With one hand she started the car, and with the other she reached for me.

"I love Italians!" she said.

My stomach muscles contracted. Say something now. *Ora!* "You love Italians. Then you love me. I am an Italian."

"Oh, certainly. I'm crazy about Italians."

Some girls from the Typewriting Class passed by to get to their car. It's winter. I am not dressed properly. I am shivering.

The perfume of this pink rose in bloom calls me.
God, how am I to know what I'm supposed to do?
My heart is the target of a thousand love arrows.
God, how am I to recover from this injured heart?

Do I let go? Do I let it be? Do I go with the flow,
Like the river to the sea and the sea to the ocean?
It's no use. I am here to struggle. My body writhes.
This beauty wants me, but I barely touched her.

It was just a caress! This is not good!

"Where do you live?" she said.

"On d'Iberville, in Ahuntsic."

"Oh, I live in St. Laurent! If not, I would bring you there!"

"I know." I know you are sweet.

"Are you okay?" she said.

"Oh, yes! Yes!"

Please, stay here! Don't let us go! Please! Let me fondle you once, twice, thrice more and again.

I writhe. I hurt. Why do you give me no rest? Why?
Speak! Speak to me, you that of these ways are the master,
Maker to ever-fleeting harmonies that drop from above
To feed nature that brings forth your fruit.

The palm of my hand is raised to you, elevates to you in praise.
Why, why do you want to smother me with your beauty?
You know I have to learn how to embrace this crushing love.
Ah, my feelings, how agonizing and painful they seems!

You keep investing me with love you pour on me from the sky,
Attacking me from all sides. I am left without defenses.
Yet, have no pity! Spare not this poor soul of mine!
See, I can resist! I can resist! Don't stop! Don't stop!

From the bottom of my soul how I beg to let this charge continue,
It could not be sweeter to me than to be your eager target!
That I be under such attack! That I be under such attack!
Let it continue! Let it continue! I beg of you. I beg of you.

Maureen! Maureen! I was wrong not to kiss you, not
to caress you, not to ravish you in your small sports
car.
   "How old are you?" she said.
   "Sixteen." I said.
   "Guess mine now!" she said.
   Clumsy! Just so clumsy! She gave me a lift to the
bus stop. *Bifolco!* Peasant!
   "You say nothing of my Italian," she said.
   "Are you going to call me, this weekend?" I said.
   "I'll phone you, if I don't go to Toronto."
   There, there, kid!
   'I hope you're not too disappointed in me.' This
was what I thought when she dropped me at the bus
stop. But I didn't tell her.

I was walking home, after I got off from the bus.
"Smiling lips don't fade away!" I murmured. "Let it be
you and I, my beauty!"

5C. My Doomed Date Liane

EVEN SO
When it comes to you,
you know, I am one-sided.
If there's disquiet in my heart,
you help me fill it with cheer.
What else, what more,
could I ask of you, love?

MENTAL PENETRATION (INSIGHT)
I was in high school at the time. It was a Saturday in October. At seven o'clock, I said to her, "I'm ready to leave." I went out with my suede coat. It was brisk. The air felt fresh in the lungs.

When I got to my bus stop, two young boys were there waiting for the bus. One boy was in a brown jacket, the other in a white raincoat. The former walked up and down to overcome the cold perhaps. They both had handsome long hair. A woman went into the store facing the bus stop, and soon came out leaving the store empty and desolate with the lady-owner behind the counter, not visible from the street. Another woman came to the door next to the store. She rang the bell, waiting. She rang again. No one came to open the door and she left. I was waiting for the bus with the two boys. A few more people passed by. I became aware that my Saturday evening in Montreal, and that of others, was about to begin.

When I was getting on the bus, I tripped. Nothing bruised except my ego. Sitting on the bus I noticed my image in the windows of the bus and a woman who was sitting in front of me with a red scarf.

Waiting for the train in the subway station, I noticed a young girl who was all alone. There were several couples that were going out. They were holding hands. I thought of pairing with the young girl who was all alone and skipping my rendezvous with **Liane**. She was less pretty but, on the upside, she was not skinny like Liane.

In the train, the tomboyish girl, sitting in front of me, was chewing gum. She reminded me of somebody. With a body so satisfying, I would have eaten her. She had one leg over the other. She showed off a superb thigh in all its grandeur. It seemed as if she wanted to seduce me. She certainly had what it took.

I stopped looking at the leg of the young girl who played with my desire, and turned my attention to the couple on my left. The young guy had his feet on the seat in front of him. His girl teased him. At times she would give him a kiss, at others a caress.

The couple at my right was standing. The boy, leaning against the train door, was hiding his girl's face with his arm. But I could see her legs and what legs they were! I remembered the legs of the young student that I had noticed at the Jean Talon subway station on coming from the French School. Just as beautiful! At a train stop I got to see the face of the girl with the beautiful legs. She had a pretty baby-like face to suck on. The tomboyish girl got off. I had an erection. I was happy I wore my long jacket. Thinking that I had been a disillusionment to the tomboyish girl, I mentally prepared myself for Liane.

Outside the subway, a couple was waiting for the bus. Two young girls and a man crossed the street to get in line with us.

On the Graham Rd. bus, I remembered about the botanical garden when I went out for the first time with

Liane. I asked the bus driver for directions. The couple got off before me.

When I got off the bus, I saw the college. I had to go to the right now. I crossed the street. An airplane passed overhead with all its noise. This was Louise's Saint Laurent. At my right, a young girl came in the opposite direction. She seemed to be possessed by fear. Finally I found Liane's house. I combed my hair with my fingers. The street was deserted. I recognized the garage doors. I was thinking about Maureen.

PHYSICAL PENETRATION (INSERTION)

I knocked at the door. I was nervous. Liane made a remark about my coat, after a kiss. The dress she was wearing was her sister's? She showed me a book of poems. We French-kissed for the first time. We undressed. There was nothing romantic about it, but it was practical. She was so skinny! I barely entered her *patanella* and I ejaculated. That was the first time, and then there was a next. I wanted to go home.

"You are not free to stay?" she said.

I called my mother to let her know that I would be home in the morning. We sat on the sofa. I wanted to know from her how to say the French 'r'. Later, I wanted to draw her.

"Get paper and pencil," I said.

"Not now," she said.

In bed we made love one more time. Or, so I thought.

"You did not penetrate, Achille," she said.

"What?"

"And, I didn't like at all when you were telling me to gain weight," she said.

I couldn't sleep. "Are you cold? Because I am." I said.

She got up to get an extra bed cover. Just before falling asleep, the noise of an airplane brought Maureen to my memory.

It was Sunday morning. I gave her a peck on the cheek.

She said, "You are sweet. Are you angry because you did not penetrate?"

At the door, I said, "Goodbye, Liane! Thank you!"

As I was waiting for the bus, I saw a small sports car driving by on the other side. What if that was Maureen?

On the way home, I conceded that, also with Annina and Anna, there had been no penetration.

5D. My Doomed Date Dominique

MY CURE
It's that body I want to possess
And I want to possess it to excess.
Oh, it's sweet to bathe in her eyes!
and to cure myself of my obsession.

SOMEONE ELSE'S TURN
I was in high school at the time. It was a summer day when a new friend of mine and I went to see a prostitute at her apartment. There, in her living room, we met an old friend of mine.

"What are doing here? You just got married," I said.

"Well, there is a difference," he said. And he gave me some lame explanation. Then, his pal came out from the bedroom. They left straightaway. On the way out, his pal was snickering. I saw them get into a Camaro parked right in front of the apartment building.

MY TURN
It was my turn. In her bedroom, she took off her nightgown to reveal a naked, well-proportioned, young body. I got undressed. I was naked in front of her. I was not aroused. I shook my penis. She smiled at first and then her smile turned into a frown. I approached her. Her body was cold. She knelt in front of him. She was gentle. In no time the desired effect was achieved.

"You're fast. Very fast." she said.

She lay on her back and opened her legs. I tried to penetrate her. I missed. I applied more pressure.

"You're hurting me," she said.

She took my penis in her hand and eased it into her loose *patana* (mature potato).

Our two bodies engaged in a machine-like movement, up and down, up and down. The phone rang. She stopped to answer the phone. After the phone call, we quickly finished our sordid affair.

Then, we had an argument because she wanted fifteen dollars. I had been told by my friends that the price ten dollars.

TURN OF EVENTS

Later, on the way home, as I was waiting for the bus with my new friend, I couldn't stop spitting. She had kissed me on the mouth! When I thought about where her mouth had been, with me and before me!

"Did you catch something, Achille?" my new friend said and he laughed. It was funny to him, not so to me. Who was he to talk? He has chickened out. It was his turn to go after me, but he didn't. He just got her phone number from her, saying he was going to see her some other time. Had I been wiser, I would've done the same thing. Anyway, I did find out from him that her name was **Dominique**.

I went there pumped and I came out deflated. Those were fifteen minutes of shame. I wanted to go back and erase them from my life. Perhaps I didn't have to ask forgiveness from God, but I certainly had to ask forgiveness from all the people who were dear to me. On the negative side, this was going to be a stain on my conduct. On the positive side, I could proudly claim that **there was penetration this time**.

6A. My Romantic Pursuit Bianca

THE MUTUAL GOOD
I'm thinking of you, today
and when I'll be away.
This isn't to say sweet things
to lure you with false feelings!
Think of the mutual good
if be in love we would.
For you I don't know how it'd be
but I know the joy you'd be to me.
My heart would jump again
like it used to do then.
Yet, there is much, much more,
that I and you so deeply adore.
In my deep adulation
I'd find my salvation!
Oh, a chance to hold you, please!
Let me hug your legs at your knees!

We landed in Montreal in mid October 1966. I was 15 at the time. That first year in Canada I didn't go to school. During the winter I worked as a house painter. They were building new houses in Saint Leonard at the time. Then, **the following year, before I started high school**, my summer job was at a factory for bedspreads. The factory was located along Chabanel Street in Ahuntsic, the garment district in Montreal.

The first time I saw **Bianca**, I had a bad impression of her. Her friend Sonia asked me for a match. I couldn't help. I didn't smoke. Then, she lighted her cigarette with her own matches.

At break time, curly-haired Michelle said to me, "Give me something to eat."

"Here," I said. I gave her my grapes.

At lunchtime, Sonia and Bianca came to see Riccardo. I was there, crouched on the table and eating my lunch.

At the beginning, I worked with Riccardo. Then, I was promoted to bedspreads cutter. At the long cutting table, Carlo was at my right and Giovanni, Bianca's friend, at my left.

One day, Giovanni, as a game, stared at her and she stared back at him for a good five minutes. I would have liked that! So, I tried to do the same thing. But she would not stare back at me. Except for this one time when she looked at me straight in the eyes. An overwhelming joy ran along my body.

"Achille loves you." Carlo said to her.

"Nothing could be further from my mind!" she answered.

I noticed that, in the evening, she took Chabanel to go home.

One morning, before work, she came where I was. She had cream in her hands and pretended to smear it on Riccardo's face. They were talking about Giovanni.

"Your friend must be fierce?" I interjected.

"Uh-uh! He's very ticklish. If I go like this, he jumps up," she said.

I laughed and I went to work with a smile on my face. I felt good. Bianca had laughed with me.

Bianca's laughter was beautiful. You'd never satisfy yourself of it. I became enamored of her mouth since the first time I saw her laughing.

I decided not to bother her anymore with the staring thing.

Having a grudge against Riccardo, Sonia flirted with a newly arrived, French-Canadian guy. Bianca was with her and this new guy. I felt cheated and began again to stare at her. One morning I looked at her straight in the eyes. She looked at the ground. I slid on the cutting table to get the rolls on the other side. I heard her say, "Sonia. He keeps looking at me. What do I do?"

So, the lady doesn't want me to look at her. Very well, I won't.

Once, she ran by me to get to her place. I had to climb over a box to avoid her bumping into me. Did she do that on purpose? I looked down. My hands were shaking.

Sonia was teasing me about her. Now, she wanted to relate to me and I didn't.

During a lunch break, I was eating and I noticed that no one was paying attention to her. I felt I had to protect her.

Later in the day, at the cutting table, I said, "I am really serious, Carlo. I don't care what she's done before. I like her."

"Oh, Achille! You care for her? She would let anyone put it in her mouth."

I brought my sketchbook to work. I was drawing during the lunch break.

"He drew a naked girl!" someone said. They came to my table to look at the drawing. Carlo proposed I draw Bianca. I looked up at her. She blushed.

I had very little time left. I was starting school soon. At the end of my last day of work, I took the elevator. It was just Bianca, a middle-aged woman, a boy, and I.

To my gratification, the boy made our downward descent longer by pressing all the buttons.

The elevator was stopping at every floor. We were coming from the fifth floor.

"It is this guy who pushed all the buttons," said Bianca. "Stop doing that!" To get him away from the buttons, she slapped on his hands.

I smiled. I was amused by what was happening.

She looked at me. The expression on her face changed. She became docile and kept staring at me, gazing at me. *What fascination could I be to her?*

I looked at her too. Straight into her eyes, those shiny, beautiful eyes that made my heart shudder every time she looked at me. I wanted this moment to last forever. I didn't want the elevator to go down. I wanted it to go up and reach the mountain peaks, the clouds, and the stars. I prayed the boy would be quiet, wouldn't move, or do something naughty and childish, as it was his nature. And what about the other woman? Her attention was on the door.

After what seemed an eternity, there was a thud. The elevator had stopped. We'd reached the ground floor.

But Bianca didn't move. She remained there, still staring at me.

I remained there too. I was waiting for her to go out first.

She did not move. *Was she waiting for me to go to her, take her hand, lead her out of the elevator to a secluded corner, and kiss her forever?*

Then, suddenly, she recovered and hasted away after the middle-aged woman.

I wish I could go back, Bianca, and do what you wanted me to do or, more precisely, do what I should have done.

6B. My Romantic Pursuit Louise

DO YOU LIKE TO MAKE FUN OF ME?

Your intentions are to mock me
When you say that to me.

Your face bursts with laughter
When you announce to me,

"Come! Here! Here!
Between my legs! Look!

Do you wanna touch?
Uh-uh, that's not for you!"

SECONDARY CHARACTERS

Giovanni	Achille's rival
Sherly	Louise's best friend
Carmine	Sherly's interest
Beverly	Louise's friend
Adam	Louise's friend
David	Louise's cousin
Maurizio	Achille's friend
Carlo	young co-worker
Giuseppe	old co-worker
Paul	factory's manager
Mauro	floor manager

After Secondary 3, when I was 17, my summer job was at a shipping factory for women's garments. The factory was located along Chabanel Street in Ahuntsic, in the garment district of Montreal.

FIRST WEEK
During my first week at the factory, I met sixteen-year-old **Louise**. She was nice, polite, and kind. She seemed to be on a quest for good deeds. *Excuse me! Thank you! Let me help you!* She was this way with everybody.

One day I drew a profile on her suntanned left thigh and another day I drew her in my sketchbook. Then she went to Boston Beach for two weeks and that halted my winning streak.

> O my God, help me.
> Let her come back to me.
> And let my love for her
> Every day greater be.

SECOND WEEK
On **Tuesday**, Carmine told me that one night he and Giovanni gave Louise and Sherly a ride home with Giovanni's car. In the car they tried to make a pass at them with no success.

This must've happened the day before I saw Carmine sitting by Louise and Sherly and this had dissuaded me from asking Louise to pose for me; but, the day after, I asked her and she posed for me.

Now the question was, "Who paired with Louise? Carmine or Giovanni?" I preferred Carmine and never that animal of Giovanni.

Carmine told me the story: "Giovanni and I met Louise and Sherly in the lobby. We gave them a ride home with Giovanni's car. We took them by the St. Lawrence Boulevard, but they didn't want to do anything. You would touch her leg and she'd say,

'Don't touch me!'. You would get closer and she would move away. When we saw that, we let them be. *Vaffá 'ncule!* So, we took them home. Bye, bye, and that's that. We had decided to go dancing before, but, after the way they behaved, everything fell apart. Now, that one, Sherly, she glares at me and I glare back at her even more. One of these days I am going to say to her, 'Hey, you! What do you want?'"

When Carmine and I got to the basement and were about to enter the cafeteria, we met a guy wearing glasses in his late twenties. Carmine called him Antonio. The guy was talking about a girl who was always calling him up at the office and she was asking for a lift. *Was this girl Louise or Sherly?* And then this guy said that he was going to tell her straight out if she wanted to fuck. Then, always talking about this, they sat on the couch. I sat beside David, Louise's cousin, who told me about Paris and compared that city to our Montreal. He also told me that Louise too speaks French. And he told me that her uncle is a millionaire.

On **Wednesday**, Carmine and I went out together at lunchtime. I found out from him that he paired with Sherly. That meant, alas, that Giovanni paired with Louise. Stupid Giovanni!

Adam, Louise's friend, offered to give me her phone number. He thought I wanted to go out with her.

On **Friday**, David told me that Louise is coming back from Boston Beach on Sunday. Adam gave me her phone number. Going home, on the stairs, he said, "I bet you're the only one who wishes it were already Monday."

THIRD WEEK

On **Monday**, I said to Adam, "Did you see my dream crumble, Adam? I stepped on coals of fire yesterday night."

I called her up at home. Her father and mother answered me. A terrible doubt rose in my mind. Louise wasn't home when I called her because she and Sherly went dancing with Giovanni and Carmine? Uneasiness in my heart prevented me from falling asleep. It was midnight. I got up. I went to the living room window and then to the washroom. I saw my face in the mirror and for a moment, that moment, I understood. *Who am I? How much am I worth?*

"You don't have a hundred hours or a hundred days, you have a hundred years. You'll remember this moment and you'll cry for no reason, and you can't go back in time." This is what Adam said to me.

Oh, could I go back in time, to yesterday night only, and not call her up at home.

On **Tuesday**, after another restless night, I found out from Carmine this morning that my doubts were wrong. She didn't go out with Giovanni yesterday night.

I gave her her drawing and with this I have given her up too. This was the end. When I asked her to pose for me again, she said, "Not today, but some other day."

When I go back to drawing, is it because I want to capture her beauty or is it because I want to show off to her?

I confided with Carmine and he offered to help me. At noon we were to go out with them, but it didn't work out the way we planned.

Louise doesn't like Giovanni. When he said something (coarse, of course) in Italian, she said, "Speak French, please!"

Tonight, when I went to bed, I had to deal with the fact that I didn't have Louise's drawing anymore. I used to look at it each night before going to sleep. I loved and cherished that drawing! The only thing left to me now was to accept and submit if I wanted to appease my heart and soul. I could not have another night like the previous one when I tormented myself. *I want her to be mine. But how much do I deserve?*

On **Wednesday**, I was sent to work on the forth floor. Later in the day, I found out that Louise was working on the same floor.

I thought of that sweet moment, that Thursday when she was leaving for her vacation in the States and I went to talk to her about her drawing. She had changed her hairdo and she was beautiful!

At noon, at the end of lunch, she was sitting on the couch with Sherly and so were Maurizio and Mario. Maurizio, my friend, made a gesture to me. I nodded. I got a glance of her. So bitter! Why does it have to be like this?

I went outside with Domenic. On coming back from our walk, from Saint Lawrence, I saw her sitting on the grass with her friends. Carmine joined us. It was late, almost one o'clock. On our way into the factory, she walked with Sherly.

For the whole afternoon, I didn't see her on the forth floor. I got a glance of her when I was going down the stairs. I went to the basement to get my jacket and didn't see her anymore, either in the lobby or outside. Did she take an earlier bus or was somebody taking her home by car?

On **Thursday,** she went out with her girlfriend at the end of lunch, but I didn't. They came back at around 12:45 and sat on the couch. I stayed at the table with Maurizio, Carlo, and two other guys. Carmine joined us later.

When I was about to go upstairs, I saw that Giovanni was sitting beside her and she was smiling. That tormented me.

At five o'clock I saw her and Sherly going on foot while I was taking the bus. Was anybody going to pick them up by car later? Giovanni and Carmine perhaps?

I like her. I like her very much. Her hair, her hair kills me.

On **Friday,** I still avoided her. In the morning I got a glimpse of her and it was marvelous.

At noon, they sat on the couch. They didn't go out. Maurizio wanted to sit on the couch where they were, but I convinced him to sit with me on the couch under the clock.

Today I had a bad cold. I went into the cloakroom to blow my nose. I met Louise and Sherly when I was coming out of the cloakroom.

Going to my table with my lunch and orangeade in my hands, I glanced in the direction of her table. She was looking towards me. At me? I lowered my head and continued on with a funny, and perhaps stupid, smile on my lips.

Carmine ate at our table. "To avoid those filthy girls," he said.

In the afternoon, I was sent to the forth floor. And, as chance would have it, I met her up there. She was about to move a cart, but I behaved as though I hadn't seen her. I paid attention to Frank, who was to get the stock I had been sent upstairs to get. *I don't look at her and then I complain when I can't see her.*

Going home at five, right when I was getting out of the factory with Maurizio and Carlo, I saw Louise and Sherly with Carmine and Giovanni standing on the sidewalk. Just before, in the afternoon, Carmine had asked me if we were going to accompany Sherly and Louise to the metro station. And, as I said no ("I have no intention of doing that."), he might have thought of Giovanni as my substitute.

I felt bad because I thought that they were going with Giovanni's car. And with this idea in my mind I walked to the bus stop with Maurizio and Carlo. I tried not to show that my heart was in anguish. As we got to the bus stop, I looked back but I couldn't see them anymore.

But, then, since a whole mob was getting on the bus, we decided to go on foot. It was Carlo who proposed to go on foot. And I agreed immediately. I wanted to see if they were going with Giovanni's car. And then I saw that Louise and Sherly were sitting in the back of a big car and an aged man sat at the steering wheel. I was so glad!

We had to pass by their car. Sherly saw me and gestured to Louise. When I passed near her car, I didn't turn towards her. *Are you thinking about me? Does that hurt you as much as it does me, my Louise?*

FORTH WEEK
On **Monday**, she had never before appeared to me as aloof as today.

This morning, on the bus, a blonde girl with a birthmark on the upper lip, I found her very appealing. Does this explain my getting away from Louise?

Today I saw her for the first time during the morning break. She was sitting on the couch. I avoided her. I looked away from her. Then I was going to change a quarter (The machine had no change.) and she approached the machine. She was smiling. I said, "Hi!" rather loudly. I thought her smile was for me, but I was wrong, because she didn't say hi back.

At noon she went out. I didn't. I sat at the table with my work friends. It was a very hot day today. We never had a day hotter than today this year. But at around noon it threatened to rain. This seemed a good reason for not going out. Carmine too sat at the table with us.

At the end of lunchtime, I noticed she was coming up the stairs. I was in front of her. I was working on the third floor. And when I got there, she and Sherly came to punch their cards. I hoped she worked on the third floor too. And I went inside without waiting in the corridor as Maurizio did. I remember when she came to punch her card and the self-confident way she laughed. Not anymore that timid fear I so loved and made my heart leap.

Louise and I were never as far apart as today. Not a glance of acknowledgement, not a gesture of courtesy. And I didn't understand why I was so apathetic to her; I almost didn't care at all. What was it the made me feel so? Was it because of the weather? Or, was it worse? Had I lost that passion I once had for her?

If there ever was to be something of good between Louise and me, this had to be done by Adam. And Adam didn't know anything about it.

At five, going down the stairs, Louise, Sherly, and David were behind me. Did David tell her something about me? She said to him, "Stop talking!"

She was taking the bus tonight. I was waiting in the bus line. She passed by with Sherly to go and take the next bus. I wanted to get a last glance of her, in the eyes, but she didn't look up.

But, something else! What does that ring she's wearing on the left ring finger mean? Does she have a boyfriend? Is she engaged?

Tomorrow I want to talk to Adam and see if he can help me.

On **Tuesday,** at lunchtime, I sat at Adam's table. I wanted to talk to him about Louise. He was doing crosswords and I didn't get the chance.

When we were going upstairs, I saw Sherly sitting on the couch with some guy (Giovanni?) and Louise was sitting on the couch with Carmine. That perturbed me. Had they switched partners? Once Carmine told me that Louise liked him.

Later, I was separating the stock when Carmine came to get the racks. He said, "Achille, your treasure was looking for you." I knew it wasn't true but it lifted my spirits.

At five, I told Adam I wanted to know if Louise liked me. He's going to find out. And he told me that she's not engaged.

Never was David as gloomy as today. Is this because of his cousin or is it because his character is like this?

On **Wednesday,** at break time, I was coming downstairs to the cafeteria and, when I got to the basement floor, I saw Sherly but I didn't see Louise. Today I was determined to not avoid her and, perhaps, say hi to her. As I was going into the cloakroom, I heard Louise's voice, "I'm going to ask you for that dime each day."

On the way back to work, circulation stopped. I stood there waiting for the circulation to resume. She came behind me and said, "Excuse me!" to somebody else who was blocking her way. Did I cause the blockage? I should've turned and looked at her but I didn't.

At noon, Louise and Sherly went out. Maurizio and I went out also. They were sitting on the grass alone. Carmine and Giovanni were with Carol and two other French-speaking girls.

On our way back I had the intention to go to them with Maurizio. But Carmine and Giovanni were there. Beverly and another girl stopped by them and then they went away. The lady from the office was also there sitting on the grass with them.

During the afternoon there was little work at packing. I hoped Paul or Mauro would come and send me to the forth floor, where I would see her and where, perhaps, I would have the chance to speak to her. *Is it ever possible that we can't be friends, Louise? I've made so many mistakes. Avoiding you was the biggest. Do Carmine and Giovanni matter so much to you? I like you, Louise! I like you so much!* But that didn't happen. What happened instead was this. Even though I had been the one who had been wishing for it, it was Maurizio and Gino who were sent to work on the forth floor.

At five I was going into the cloakroom to get my jacket and she was coming out of the cafeteria. When I got outside with my sketchbook in my hand, I saw her and Sherly in that big car right in front of the factory with the aged man (probably her father) at the steering wheel. I flanked the car. I then turned and I saw her looking towards Sherly, perhaps to avoid looking at me? I was taking the bus. From inside the bus, I looked for the car again but it was gone.

Adam didn't tell me anything yet about Louise liking me.

It seems I was wrong about David. He came to the second floor and greeted me, "Achille!" And I answered him, "Hello!"

I went to the Sauve Park with Tony tonight and I told him about my Louise story.

Everything went wrong with Louise since the phone call, but I was mostly upset about the fact that we couldn't even greet each other. I never got a sign of encouragement from her so that I might say hi to her. But now it seemed too late to go back and repair the damage done, or was it? Perhaps it was like Tony said. "She's shy like you."

I want you, Louise! Why can't we find a means of communication, an understanding that is dear to both of us?

On **Thursday** morning, I left home with the resolution of talking to Louise alone and I hoped to have a chance like yesterday. I regretted I didn't do it yesterday when she was outside in front of the factory. I could've approached her and then I would've asked her, "Do you like me?" This is what I thought about this morning on my way to the factory.

When I got to the factory it was early and I got a chance of talking to David. I couldn't resist the temptation of asking him about Louise.

"No!" said David. "We haven't talked about you since the day she left for Boston Beach. No. I don't think she likes you." This was a statement that rang in my ears all morning long.

"How can you tell?"

"Because I know Louise and I know that if she likes somebody, she sticks with him. Since the day she came back, I have never seen you two together once."

"Yes, but you don't know what I did to her. I didn't even look at her."

David nodded. We rose to go upstairs. I wanted to continue but David left me to go and say hi to a friend of his. It was pretty obvious I annoyed him.

I was going upstairs and I saw Sherly who was about to come in. I kept looking at her and then Louise came in and she looked up at me. I imagined the following conversation: "Why did you look at me?" she would say. "And why did you look at me?" I would say.

Upstairs I met Adam. I was talking to him but he didn't say a word about what he'd promised to find out. I then finally asked him about it. He was trying to find excuses and then he said, "Forget it. If she liked you, she would have shown it when you gave her the picture. You didn't have to give her the picture. She doesn't deserve it."

I received his last statement with a snap of the fingers and some repressed laughter. What roundabout flattery!

After all this, I passed a morning oppressed by disheartening and depressing thoughts. I felt rejected. I felt the loss of what I cared the most in life. Everything else was not important. Nothing in life was worth anything. All this sadness!

After these thoughts, I wondered about the workings of the human mind. If one fails to see the beauty of life, one succumbs to ugliness. I chose beauty and expelled those ugly thoughts from my mind. *She's not the only girl in the world!*

After lunch, I went out with Maurizio. He wanted to be with Carol. Louise and Sherly were already outside on the grass with Carmine and Giovanni. I shunned her and them. We went where Carol was. In the meantime I wrecked my brains about Louise. On our way back I still shunned her but when I got in the lobby of the factory, I couldn't resist looking back and I saw that she was getting up. She seemed to look my way. As we were going up, I told Maurizio about my problem.

In the afternoon, Mauro sent me to the forth floor to bring Paul a cart of cartons. My heart trembled when I got there. I saw David. But my time up there was too short to see if she was there.

Later, Linda asked me to show her a red garment I was packing. I was shaking. I couldn't control myself. I feared she and Maurizio would notice. I quieted my uneasiness by thinking that beauty is my lifetime goal. As I said to Tony last night, Linda, physically, is the most perfect woman I have ever met in my life. Oh, had she been half as perfect in that little head of hers! Nevertheless, every male in the factory, young and old, goes into ecstasy when she's around. Notwithstanding, if I'd been told to choose between Linda and Louise, I would've chosen Louise hands down.

At five I was in the staircase and was about to reach the basement when I met Louise and Sherly, who were coming up to go out. Certainly as a joke, Sherly said, "Hi!" I turned and I also said, "Hi!" rather loud and it was more of a growl than a greeting. While I reached the cloakroom, I heard the sound of laughter at my back. And now I had the doubt that that "Hi!" was not directed at me. Anyway, I should not have had such doubts because what I did was spontaneous, without artifice, with sincerity. I did what

I believed the situation demanded of me at the moment.

When I got outside, my friend Dario greeted me. "Over here, Achille!" he said. I saw Louise and Sherly waiting at the bus stop. In part I was happy to join Dario and avoid perhaps another embarrassing situation at the bus stop. Dario wanted to go and meet his girlfriend at work and I went with him. We talked about Linda. Dario was the hero who had gone out with Linda, when he had worked at the shipping factory a couple of years back.

On **Friday,** I got the chance I'd been longing for. Anyhow, I was unprepared for the way it happened.

In the morning I didn't see Louise, and, at the break, I shunned her completely. I didn't even try to look at her. However, after the break, Paul sent Maurizio, Carlo, and me to work on the forth floor, right where she was with Beverly, David, Christine, and two other guys. And I didn't say a word till noon, except to Maurizio. There were some jokes. She said "Thank you!" to me once, at the beginning.

"You don't talk?" said Christine to me.

"I don't understand French very well," I said, but the real reason was not a matter of language.

At lunch she wasn't in the cafeteria. Later, Carmine, Maurizio, and I went outside. She wasn't there too. I didn't know where Louise and friends, including Adam, went to have their lunch.

I wanted Maurizio to explain why he didn't tell me that he had worked with Louise on the forth floor the day before. But it wasn't true. And it was also not true what happened with David. Before lunch, I had just got on the forth floor, when Beverly ordered David to shut up as I arrived. It seemed he wanted to tell me something about Louise.

That afternoon was very important to me. I finally broke the ice that I had built around me and which seemed now unbearable. I did it. I broke the ice.

I was asking David about what they were talking about before, when Louise approached us and said, "What is it?"

"Nothing," I said.

But David told her everything.

"No. We weren't talking about you. I swear," she said.

Later, I started to talk to Beverly. She had a very likable character and we bonded.

During the problem of the misplaced slip, Beverly said, "Oh, you speak English?"

"Yes, I do," I said.

"And do you speak Italian also?"

"Yes, *meglio di te.*"

"What does *bongiorno* mean?" Beverly asked Louise.

"*Buonasera,*" I said.

"Hey, Sherly," Louise said. "I'm going to be Beverly's maid of honor when she marries."

"And I'm going to be the best men," said David.

"I want to be a maid of honor too," lamented Sherly.

I'm going to be there too, I thought of saying. *I'm going to be the groom.*

Somebody shipped Beverly's box. "That person might have been me," I told her. I was pretty worried about it and I thought I had done the mistake. I even had a box of mine brought back to the forth floor, but it was not necessary. That and my defending her with Paul enhanced my brief, but not futile, friendship with her.

And it was a pity that today was Beverly's last day of work. I asked Louise if this was her last day of work also. She said no.

"Hi!" Sherly said, when she was close to me.
"Hi!" I said.
"How are you?"
"Very well. Thank you." Christine laughed. Then, I took courage and said, "Carmine was very sad this afternoon. Did you *fire* him?"
"No! He's a nice guy."
"I know."

David told me that, when Beverly told him to shut up, he was about to tell me what a dirty guy Giovanni was. It seemed that, in the end, Louise had understood that he was no good.

After the shipping was done, Gaetan and I were putting in order the stock and Louise and David were working on the other side.

I was placing the stock on the last shelf of the cart. Gaetan and David were further away.
"Well, Louise," I said. "Did you hang my Mona Lisa?"
At first she did not understand. And then with a gesture she understood I meant my drawing of her.
"Yes, I hung it with my other pictures," she said.
"You did?"
"Yes!"
"Uh-uh! I don't believe you."
David came and said, "Hey, Achille, draw me." And he made a pose, a mock pose.
"When I become well known like Picasso, I will," I said.

There were laughs and a great deal of jokes about *maccheroni* and the Arabic phrase *Is you mother cute?*

"Because your grandfather was Italian, are you also a *maccheroni*?" I said to Louise. She laughed. She didn't understand what I was talking about. "Your last name is Italian," I added.

"How do you know my last name?"

"How do I also know your phone number?"

"Who gave you my phone number?"

"Adam?" said David.

"I'm not allowed to tell," I said.

"Oh, look, my last name is a secret now!" she said.

"Your last name is not a secret, but it is a secret about who told me," I said.

"Ah!"

"Do you want her phone number?" said David.

"I have it. I got it because I thought I needed it."

Louise seemed to have made a mistake about a box she had shipped. Mauro told her. She went and checked. Her mother and Paul got there. Paul was teasing her. "Come on. Tell your mother that you have a boyfriend."

"Yes, I do," she said and it seemed to me she said that to put an end to the teasing.

Before, while we were shipping, she was telling David, "I am not going out with anybody." At that moment, I was tempted to say, 'I'm ready to go out with you.' but I didn't.

Later, Mauro made Gaetan, a French-speaking girl, and me put the remainder stock into boxes right beside where Louise and Sherly were working. They were ticketing the stock.

Now that Louise had acquired a great deal of confidence with me, each time I passed by to go and get the boxes under the bench on which they worked, she said, "Hi!"

On the third time, I said, "Hi!" too and then added, "Do you like to make fun of people?"

"What?" she exclaimed.

Sherly came to her defenses. "Why! If you don't want her to say hi to you, she won't do it anymore. She was only being kind."

"Don't get angry now," I said. "I just asked a question."

"She was only trying to be nice," said Sherly.

"Why this late?"

"You mean why she didn't say hi to you before?"

"Yes, why this late?"

Right at that moment Beverly got there and she asked what time it was. I told her it was 4:10. And I left with the boxes.

I went to get the boxes another couple of times and not a word was uttered. Once, Beverly pretended shooting at me with the price gun in her hand and I smiled at her. I thought of saying to her, 'Why don't you shoot Louise?' just to make a joke and return to the pleasant agreeableness of before.

She was finally talking to me. And I behaved like a dork. I wrecked it! I wrecked what I had been craving for all along. Just because she was teasing me!

I went to the washroom. I thought about what I had done. I resolved of going to her and telling her how much I had wanted her to say hi to me. But, when I got back to work, I was no longer hopeful with my resolution.

In the washroom I also realized that time was running by. It was going to be five o'clock soon. So, I believe, it was the second time I went to get the boxes that I got the chance to look at her and she looked back at me. "Hi!" I said.

"Don't make fun of her!" Sherly said.

"She doesn't like it?" I said by addressing Sherly.

"You didn't like it, either," Sherly said.

"I liked it!" I protested. "I liked it!"

And when I went back again, I addressed Louise, "Did you understand?"

It was Sherly who answered for her, "She understands. Oh, yeah, she understands. Don't worry."

"Good," I said.

"She doesn't want to make fun of you, Achille," Beverly said.

Holding the boxes high in my hands, I was in front of the ventilator, I turned and I said, "Me neither." At this point, I wanted to say, 'The fact is, Beverly, that I like her, I like her so much.'

"Then everything is the way it was before," Sherly said.

"Yeah," I answered as I was going away.

After this, in the other couple of times I went to get the boxes, nobody uttered a word or stole a glance.

Then, it was 4:50 and I went to find Maurizio where he worked with Carmine, Carlo, and David. I was very boisterous and jovial, perhaps more than I usually was. Was this euphoria due to the fact that I had finally been speaking to Louise? Maurizio was nice as ever and David was as cordial as he had ever been. At 4:55 we left and there was a final joke when Carmine asked what time it was. Maurizio said there were only five minutes left, David said four, and I said three.

On the way down, in the staircase, I saw Louise again with Beverly and Sherly. They were about a flight of stairs ahead of us. Sherly was saying to everybody, "Come and say goodbye to Beverly. She is leaving. This is her last day of work." Sherly saw Carmine and told him about Beverly. He seemed to be cross with her but she conquered him in no time with her affable manners.

Outside I saw them again. Sherly was still announcing Beverly's leave. I wanted to really say goodbye to Beverly. She'd been very nice to me. But I just passed by and joined Maurizio who was waiting for me beside the sidewalk on the grass.

Again I thought of going and saying goodbye to Beverly with Maurizio. We would have kissed Beverly goodbye. And then I would have asked Louise, 'Are you leaving too? This might be the only way I can get a kiss from you.' My joke would have cheered her up and she would have had a good memory of me over the weekend.

I took the bus and I thought Louise and Sherly were going by car as they had other times. In the bus I sat in the back. As the bus started, I looked for them in that big car but I didn't see the car or them. Then, looking at the people who went on foot towards St. Lawrence Boulevard, I saw Louise, Sherly, and Carmine. Carmine had his right arm around Sherly's shoulders. As the bus passed by, I didn't look back not to be seen by them. But later I regretted I hadn't. I wished I had looked at her and perhaps waved at her, to leave her with some sweetness and not with the bitterness I had shown her.

For a moment it seemed to me that Giovanni was there beside *my* Louise. The bus stopped at the red light. I got a good view of them. No Giovanni! It was just the three of them. I had the thought of getting off and joining them; but what would I tell them? Wouldn't that have seemed odd? I didn't get off.

Now, in hindsight, I know I should've got off the bus and said to her, "I liked so much you teasing me. I was cocky. I was a dork. I should've never said to you what I did. I take it back. I want you to tease me. Keep on teasing me. Make fun of me, if you want. But don't stop talking to me."

Later, at home, I thought of phoning her, talking to her, asking her to go out with me during the weekend. But that might have been another gaffe of mine and might have complicated things even more like the time I called her and her mother answered. And so I refrained myself again.

On **Saturday** morning I thought about how much I wanted her, how much I suffered for her. In the afternoon, I went to play soccer at Jarry Park with Tony, Frank, Domenic, and Patrick. We found Jimmy and his brother-in-law there.

On **Sunday,** a rainy day at the end, I went to Pointe Calumet Beach with Tony, Maurizio, Carlo, and Patrick.

On the beach, Carlo made the others notice how I was always thinking. Maurizio reminded me of Louise. I thought about her all day. And that was what I was thinking about when Carlo pointed that out that I was lost in thought. Two weeks before, when we went to that same beach, I was also thinking about her. At that time she was supposed to come back from vacationing in the States. Those were hopeful thoughts; today's thoughts were not.

I hope I don't disappoint you, tomorrow, Louise. Oh, I so much want you. Help me, my God!

FIFTH WEEK

On **Monday,** I wanted to talk to her and I had to do it now because I might not get too many chances, as this was her last week at the factory.

I want to talk to you! What is the matter? I don't see what the whole problem is. Do you like me, Louise? I like you. I like you so much.

This morning I saw her for the first time when I was going upstairs and she was waiting for the elevator. This was not a good chance for what I had resolved to tell her.

She was working on the second floor. When she came in and was going towards the shipping area, I was with Maurizio. I called her, "Hi, Louise!" I called her again but she didn't seem she'd heard me. "Do you want me to call her?" said Maurizio. He called her. She turned. Maurizio said hi and I nodded with my head.

At break time I wanted to approach her and say to her, 'Are you still mad at me for what happened on Friday?' But I didn't get an iota of encouragement from her.

After the break, as chance would have it, I was sent by Paul to the forth floor to work with Maurizio and Orlando. That's exactly what I had wished for this morning, but now, regrettably, she happened to work on the second floor.

Anyway, Sherly was there. The second time I looked at her she smiled. That was comforting.

At noon I saw that Louise and Sherly were chatting with Mike at Giovanni's table. Mike was quite handsome and I could see why girls were attracted to him. But, Mike was more interested in playing cards with the boys.

Carmine passed by us. My table companions commented on his hair. Maurizio, Antonio, and I got up to go out. I wanted to ask Maurizio to help me with Louise, but Antonio was with us. Perhaps it was better so. I didn't think it was a good idea to rely on other people in matters of the heart. It was on me and me alone.

When we got outside, she was sitting on the grass. Adam and friends were there too. Carmine lay with his head in Sherly's lap. Louise was talking with some guy I had never seen before. I was very troubled by that. I wanted to have a chance to speak to her.

At 12:45 we went back in. Maurizio went into the office to make his daily phone call to his girlfriend, Laura.

Maurizio and I were going upstairs. We were by the third floor when we saw Louise coming out onto the second floor landing. Maurizio and I looked at each other for just a moment and then I leaned on the railing and said, "Hi!"

"She doesn't like it," I said to Maurizio to whom I had explained the whole story.

"Yeah, but she smiled," said Maurizio.

"Yup. It is funny," I said.

Sherly was working on the forth floor. I didn't get the chance but I imagined of asking her, 'When is your last day of work? What grade are you starting in September? Can you help me with Louise?'

At 5:00 I saw them going down the stairs in front of me. They went through the cafeteria door and that was the end of it. I hoped they would take the bus. I just saw Carmine and Domenic who were going on foot. Most probably, Louise and Sherly went by car.

On **Tuesday,** Louise said, "In this place, some people get jealous. In this place, some people act as if they own you just because you talked to them a few times. They mistake friendship for something else."

Yes, Louise. You're right. I mistake friendship for something else. You're the one who's right. But I would not be feeling this way if you had not lit again that fire in me by starting that game of yours (saying hi to me each time I came by), which ended up in the worst manner possible. I had come to understand *my* Louise. Those nice gestures and that attitude of kindness of hers, which I had fallen in love with, were altogether revealed to me in another light. I was the one to blame anyway. It was I who saw more-than-friendship where it was not. But, what were all those looks about? Why did she look each time at me? In a moment of rage, I will say, 'Look at how irrational you are!'

This morning, when I was on the couch in the cafeteria, Louise and Sherly were already there. Louise came from the cloakroom. I looked at her and she smiled. I said hi but I received no answer.

It was time to go upstairs. I waited on the couch. They passed by. I was looking at her. I wanted, I waited for a sign to say hi to her. But nothing! She passed straight by. Not even deigning me a glance. She's determined to avoid me. Sherly took her by the shoulders to guide her through the cafeteria door.

I looked at the time and I followed. They were waiting for the elevator. I looked for it but I did not get a chance of saying hi to her.

The only time she looked towards me was when she entered the second floor door. I was with Carlo and another guy and I was laughing about something. I stopped laughing immediately when I saw her.

At break time, since she was working on the second floor, I wanted to wait up for her to tell her that I wanted to speak to her alone at noon; but then I saw her with all the other girls and I did not have the guts to do what I had resolved to do. When I entered the cafeteria, she was at the buffet. And, while eating, I tried to look at her once. Just before, some guy, some new arrival, was sitting at her place, but when I turned to look again, I saw he had moved to the next table and she was sitting in her usual place.

At noon I wanted to wait for her just like before at break time. This time I was more determined than ever. The bell was about to ring and I was going to go where she worked. But the bell rang before I expected it. Adam was there and I went with him downstairs. There was nothing else to do if I did not want to be seen odd. Anyway, on our way downstairs, I told Adam, "Will you, please, tell Louise that I want to speak to her. Anyway, if I see her myself, I tell her." I waited for her downstairs for a while, but then I thought it was better to approach her at the end of lunch and so I did, after having informed myself with Adam to see if he'd given her my message. He hadn't. I approached her by the cloakroom when they were on their way out.

"Are you still mad at me for the way I spoke on Friday?" I said.

"Why, no!" She laughed and then she turned to look elsewhere.

I went with them outside the cafeteria and in the corridor I said, "I want to speak to you... alone."

"Why?" she said and she was going away.

"Don't be childish," I said.

"I'm not being childish. If you want to tell me something, say it out loud. I am with my friends. I am not embarrassed." Sherly, Rita, and Maria were there too.

They were going outside. Carmine appeared next to me and asked, "Well?" he said. I told him. We followed the girls.

"You finally made up your mind," said Carmine.

"Yeah, and, when I do it, it's either words or blows." Sherly was there and she heard me, but she didn't understand Italian. "Why do look at me like that?" I said to her. "Are you mad at me too?"

"There is something wrong with this guy," she said.

Outside, Adam asked me to sit on the grass with them. He was doing a crossword puzzle. I made another attempt to convince her to come with me. Adam tried to persuade her too.

"Adam!" said Sherly. "Perhaps she doesn't want."

Carmine was sitting on the grass not too far away from us.

"In this place, some people get jealous," said Louise. "In this place, some people act as if they own you just because you talked to them a few times. They mistake friendship for something else."

Of course, she was talking about me.

Adam's 'ex-wife' (so we called her), David, Rita, two Italian guys (one of whom Louise liked), and Giovanni were there.

"He's a nice guy, if he weren't too touchy with his hands," Louise said about Giovanni. She gave me the impression she liked Giovanni.

Giovanni stretched his clutches towards her legs. She got angry. "Don't touch me! Keep your hands to yourself!"

"Can't I have five minutes of your time? Is your time that precious?" I said.

"No! What do you need privacy for? I'll tell anyway. I'm not embarrassed."

"Maybe you're not embarrassed but I am. And I can't tell what I want to tell you in front of all these people."

Adam came to my help with the result of becoming enemies with her.

"I'm getting mad at you, Adam!" Then she said, "I'm going out with a guy." It was a complete lie.

When I told this to Carmine, on the stairs, he said, "Eh, she goes out with everybody that one!"

Today I got to know Louise better. This is not the soul I fell in love with. Or, did I just fall in love with her beautiful legs, like Giovanni? She'd seemed to be interested in me! What were all those looks about?

Wednesday morning was a normal morning except that, when she entered the second floor, she didn't look in the direction of my packing table as she used to do on other mornings. She came in by looking straight into the other direction and joined Adam whom I'd just been talking to.

During the morning nothing happened to upset my mind; but, at break time, when Adam and I were going downstairs, he said to me, "Louise told me to tell you that she apologizes for the way she acted yesterday."

"Perhaps, I have to apologize to her for upsetting her," I said.

After the break, I thought about what Adam had told me and a new hope arose in me. Perhaps, not all of it was lost! If she was apologizing to me for the way she behaved on Tuesday, this meant that she cared for me. And I imagined that on Tuesday night, at home, she had thought about me, as I had done so many nights, and she had realized how much I wanted her. A new opening for hope presented itself to me. Oh, how sweet it was!

But I was completely wrong. At the end of lunch, I had the chance to talk to Adam again. He was about to go out with Jeff.

"You know, you made me think about what you told me about Louise. What does it mean?"

"Oh, Achille, it doesn't mean anything. You see, when you left yesterday, I told her that she didn't have to act the way she did with you. And she gave me permission to apologize to you."

"Then, it's your apology, not hers!"

"No, you see ..."

And Adam tried to explain but it was useless, because now I understood what happened. The thought of apologizing had not originated from Louise, but rather forced onto her. Adam had realized he had made a 'mistake' and he wanted to cover it up but I didn't pay attention to him, because I felt so much the loss of my renewed hope.

In the afternoon, I fell into the bitterness of despair that contrasted intensely with the sweetness of hope I had felt in the morning.

Many times before I had wished for the chance to work with Adam, so I could talk to him about Louise. And, today, when I had nothing to say to him, I was sent where he worked. Carlo, Giuseppe, and Giovanni were there too.

Thursday morning seemed to begin normally. There were no worries in my thoughts. But, when I looked behind me, I saw Louise. She was shipping with old Giuseppe. I had been shipping there the night before with Giuseppe, Carlo, and Giovanni.

There wasn't too much work in packing. I wished I would be sent to work where she worked. I wanted to show her I bore no grudges. I wanted to get a chance to be nice to her. But this was highly improbable. All the same, my wish became more persistent and real in my mind, until my wish became reality. My heart was pounding when Paul send me to work where she worked. Now I had the chance I had wished for!

When I got near her I uttered a hoarse "Hi!" She answered with an angry "Hi!"

I started working in all haste. She was working in front of me. I needed a No. 10 box and went to get it. She needed the same box and she asked Giuseppe, who, very politely, went to get it for her. I would have liked she had asked me! I would have done it for her!

I finished with my box before she did. I went to get the clipper at her left. When I was about to put it back I wanted to pass it on to her but she didn't need it at that moment. And so I lost my chance to be nice to her!

When I was getting the boxes, I was conscious of her. I once looked at her, on purpose, to prove to myself that I was not shy. And another time she came very close to me for no apparent reason. I was trying to convince myself that, after all, I was the man. But I knew she was in a better position than me. I was the man yes, but she was the one who rejected me.

Then, all too quickly, she was gone. It took me sometime to realize that she had left. She had gone to make tickets or attach them to the stock. My chance to be nice to her did not last long!

At lunchtime, she went outside. I stayed inside. I sat on the couch alone. Maurizio was absent. Then I went to get my sketchbook to write about chances. I also started two small sketches. She came back with her friends and went straight into the cloakroom. I hurried up with my sketches. I didn't want her to see me drawing.

After lunch, I was working with Carlo. She passed by and said, "Bonjour!" It was directed to Carlo, which had all the looks of antagonism directed at me. I was sitting right there with the clipper in my hand.

On **Friday**, in the morning, she came in with the tickets lady. She wore a new dress. Just when I intended not to think of her, telling myself that there are so many other girls, she shows up prettier than ever in that greenish mini dress. It agreed with the white-and-red-striped sweater I wore. I liked her even more today on her last day of work.

Towards the end of lunch, I was sitting beside Michel on the couch and she, ever appealing in the dress she was wearing, came from outside with her friends. They sat at a table where she used to have lunch. The curly-haired Italian guy was there too with David and Peter and the other Italian student. They were boisterous and cheerful. Louise seemed to be the liveliest in the group. From where I was sitting, I could only see her curly hair. I gave a look at my watch and decided to go upstairs. I had to escape the torment I was in.

Going upstairs I noticed, two flights down, Carmine with Sherly. They were just coming in. I thought of that first time we went to the beach. How I felt a winner more than anybody else there, because the next day Louise was coming back to work!

In the afternoon, there was little work at packing. Carlo and I were unloading the boxes from the carts. She had gone to the washroom. Carlo had maneuvered somehow the carts and blocked off the way.

"What are doing?" I yelled at Carlo.

When Louise came back, Adam told her to walk on the conveyer. To unblock the way, I pulled one cart to move it out of the way and, in so doing, the other one moved slightly backwards. I had not noticed that she had approached from the other side to move the cart herself. When the cart moved, she backed away and shouted, "Take it easy!" It was as if she had whipped me. But I only wanted to be kind to her! I had taken today's carts incident as an opportunity to be kind to her.

'I am very sorry if I scared you. I wanted to let you through,' I wanted to tell her. But, as on other occasions, I didn't. I just stood there, waiting for her to pass, with a smile on my lips. Adam, once more, was telling her that she could've walked on the conveyer.

I was packing. It was 4:20, when Sherly and David, coming from upstairs, came to the second floor. David said hi. I shook his hand and wished him good luck. He was leaving too. Sherly and Louise pretended to be in mourning for leaving the factory.

It was about 4:25. I was separating the stock with all the gang of packers. Louise and Sherly were leaving. They said bye, on the other side first, where Louise had been working lately. They came on this side to go out of the door. Sherly said bye and then Louise. Carlo, leaning on the pile of boxes, waved his hand in a mocking manner. Louise, as moved by a second thought, came back and showed herself a little better from behind the pile of boxes and said bye again and again. Twice! Was one of those goodbyes for me?

I pictured her coming straight to me among that multitude of packers and saying to me, "Bye, Achille!". For a moment I arrogantly expected my thought to come through. I stood there. I could not bring myself to wave at her or even mouth a silent goodbye with all those men around! I was frustrated, forlorn, and fragmented. In self-defence, I turned my back and continued working.

6C. My Romantic Pursuit Amalia

DRAWING AMA
O Ama, do you remember
the initial time, when you,
worshipped and fragile flower
and dear flame in my hand were?
and anguish and torture of my soul,
assailing dream, aloft aspiration?
I know it was I,
but my cry?
Flowed my pencil
along your shoulder, free.
Ah, why? I wanted that lipstick
to be used for me!
The last stabs in my spine;
but, aw! Did you know?
Did I ache? Did I pine?
Yet, avoid you cannot
being happy and free
to subdue to my pencil.
I'll draw you, and mine
will be what was thine.

SECONDARY CHARACTERS

Gianni	Achille's rival
Mr. York	factory owner
Mr. Knight	factory manager
Paul	Mr. Knight's nephew
Mason	middle age employee
Maria	middle age employee
Mina	Maria's older daughter
Mia	teenage employee
Sonia	young adult employee

After Secondary 4, in 1969, when I was 18, during the summer, I worked in a textile factory. The factory was located along Chabanel Street in Ahuntsic, on the first floor of a three-story building.

AUGUST 25
On opening the door and coming out of the machine room, Franco said, "You drew **Amalia**?"
    "Yeah!" I said.
    "I've seen it. It's nice!"
    Had Amalia kept her drawing at the factory? Hadn't she brought it home? She had shown it to Franco. That meant she liked it. Franco had made me happy. I didn't ask him when he'd seen the drawing.

AUGUST 30
It was about 12:30. I went and looked for her. She wasn't at the shipping door in the back. So, I went to the bench where she worked and where I expected her to be. Gianni was there too. He was sitting at Mr. Quinn's desk and on the phone. Amalia was standing in the doorframe and looking at Gianni. For a while I watched them, or rather, I watched her. Then, I leaned with my elbows on the bench and jokingly I called out at him, "Hey, Mr. Quinn!" She laughed.
    I went inside the bench and I said, "Pose for me?" She pouted and agreed to pose.
    I remember the second time she posed for me. I remember my eagerness and my haste in tearing, in bending pieces of cartons on which I wanted to rest my drawing paper. In moving a box full of bobbins, the box opened at the bottom and the bobbins splattered

all over. I was in a hurry to fix the box and put the bobbins back in it. She rose and came and helped me.

This time, I had her pose with her profile to me, facing away from the light. I chose the profile view because it is easier to do, but her profile was to my right and therefore difficult for someone right-handed like me. I didn't want her to turn around. I would've had her face against the light. She took off her glasses. Like the second time I drew her, she had her hair in pigtails.

I delineated the head, going lightly to outline the forehead, semi-covered by the equally-parted hair; with the nose, I was afraid to make it ugly; then, the sweet lips I never kissed; the chin; the neck; the perfect ear; the big left eye, the eyelash of the right eye, the arching eyebrow; and the more I drew, the more I studied her, the more her features belonged to me. Her mouth was mine, her chin was mine, her neck was mine, …

I noticed Gianni at my back, scrutinizing my drawing. He said something but I didn't catch what it was. But who cared? I was drawing her neck – my pen flowed freely, going from one motion of my hand, from the nape of her neck to the end of her left shoulder; and I felt great, magnified, superior, a giant capable to crush "insects" that stood in my way, my way to get to Amalia. I drew the other shoulder and the opening of her blue blouse, pointing to the middle of her breasts. And the mammalian bust began to take form.

Gianni went away. Amalia continued posing for me lazily and bored and sleepy. I talked to her to keep her interested because I needed more time. "Are you sleepy?" because I need to better shade the corner of your eye. "Don't be too serious, now!" because I need to better define the wide nostril. "Come on, now! Don't be lazy!" because I need to better draw that smile line that winds from your nose and ends above the corner of your mouth.

When I finished the drawing, she rose and went straight to work.

"Don't you want to see it?" I said and handed her the drawing. She took it and examined it at length. She raised it and put against the light. Then, not satisfied, she took another sheet of paper, placed it in front of the drawing, and raised it again against the light. Now, she looked pleased. During all this process, she didn't utter a word and it was intriguing to watch her.

Gianni was fixing the yarn machine, when I went to the bathroom to take my shirt off. Maria, Mia, and Sonia were there. Gianni saw me, smiled, and asked, "Did you finish the drawing?"

"Yes and no," I said. "I would like to continue, if there is a chance."

And the artist, meaning me, made his way to the washroom proud and smiling.

That evening, when the three of us (Amalia, Gianni, and me) came out of the factory, we were received by a beautiful sunset. A warm red sun had barely sunk its sphere behind the elevated rail tracks. It had blooded the nearby sky and clouds. A lone poplar tree obstructed the view and that intensified the scene. It was a scene that encouraged you to dream, hope, and think of a happier future.

"Ah! Look!" I was talking to Gianni. "Don't tell me that you don't like the sunset tonight? Isn't it beautiful?"

"Ugh! And what good is that to you?" he said and continued walking.

"Oh, come on! Don't tell me that is not beautiful now?" I said to him. Because Amalia had continued walking and couldn't see the sunset from where she was, I said, "Come and see, Amalia!" She paced back. "Isn't it nice?"

"Yeah!" she said without enthusiasm. But, by the way she stared at it, I could tell she liked it. But she would not encourage me with my excitement.

I lingered a little behind and when I caught up with them, I said to Gianni, "You have to know that is not a sunset against the sky but, rather, a sunset on a painted canvas."

"Ha ha! A painted canvas!" He found what I had said ridiculous.

Past Port Royal Street, Gianni was telling us about the trade school he went to in Italy to learn to be a machine tool operator. "The school was in Benevento. You could learn to be a machine tool operator, a plumber, or an electrician. They'd pay for the trip, and they'd feed you. One day they'd make pasta and beans, another pasta and vegetables, and another pasta and potatoes.

"Did you have to go to middle school first to go to trade school?" I asked.

"Yes, but there were those who had gone only to elementary school and those who had never gone to school at all."

I wanted to ask, 'What about you?' But I didn't.

We were at the bus stop by now. The bus was coming. Amalia was by the bus stop, Gianni and I a little behind. "Did you look at Amalia?" I said. "She didn't have lipstick on, this morning. Look!

Gianni looked at her. She blushed.

"It's very chic!" I said.

"Chic?" he said.

On the bus, the conversation revolved again about Gianni's trade. "I can't work as a machine tool operator here because I don't know the English measurement system."

"It's not difficult," I said. "You have the yard, the foot, and the inch."

"Yes, but you have to know the parts the inch divides into. It's difficult," he said and hardened his chin.

Amalia had turned her face and looked outside the window. I continued talking to Gianni and, from time to time, I stole a glance at Amalia making it as normal as possible. I got off the bus at Lille. She just nodded to my "Bye!"

SEPTEMBER 1

In the afternoon I sat before the machine room on a box full of bobbins. Both parts of the machine room door were wide open and I drew on two white sheets of typing paper which rested on a board I had taken from inside the machine room and to draw I used a pencil I had borrowed from Mason. I drew two heads in the act of kissing. I sketched Rocco who was taking down the bobbins from the nylon machine. Amalia went to the washroom and, as she was passing by, on the way back from the washroom, I called her back and, pointing to the kissing heads, I said, "Look! This is you!" She shook her head. "Oh, yes!" I said nodding. She was amused and I was happy.

Later that day, I was talking with Franco, by the phone. Amalia was passing by and heading for the washroom. "Hey!" I said. "You're kidding nobody! Where do you think you're going? It's still ten to seven!" She was amused and I was happy because she was amused. To all that Franco had just been a witness. (Give me a scepter and I'll be the best of kings; give me a shovel and I'll be the worst of stable boys.)

I told Franco that I had to go and rushed to the washroom. "Wait for me!" I told Gianni, and I began dressing in a hurry. When I got to the punch clock, they were just punching. Gianni seemed uneasy. "Are we going?" I said.

"This way!" he ordered. He went back towards the workshops. I thought this was a short cut by the back. I trailed behind them. When we got at the fence, Gianni muttered something and opened the gate with his key. I waited for him and Amalia to go through and then I followed. I noticed that Gianni had two paper-wrapped bundles under his arm. We descended the iron ladder to our left to pass through the uncared for alley flanking the factory building. As we got in the alley, Amalia took a bundle from Gianni.

I said jokingly, "Cloth, eh?"

"Shh! Now don't..." he said.

"Who cares?" I assured him and we walked in queue, Amalia first, Gianni second, and I last. As we beat a footpath in this abandoned alley, I was entertained by Amalia's footwork as she was trying to avoid the tall weeds.

(What was disturbing wasn't the fact that they were stealing but the fact that they made such a fine pair of delinquents. If there can be harmony with such matters, why couldn't there be more?)

When we got in front of the factory Gianni said addressing Amalia, "What if Mr. York (the owner of the factory) would arrive now?" and imitating his rough voice, "Where are going with my cloth?" Amalia didn't find the joke too funny, considering that she barely smiled.

While waiting for the bus, Gianni sat on a projection of the bank building. Amalia leaned by the bus sign and looked directly at the other bank across the street, and I had a chance to steal a hidden, casual glance at her perfectly proportioned figure. The right arm came down beautifully, starting from the shoulder and it was curvaceous and seductive, that same arm that was going to quiver in my hand.

SEPTEMBER 8

At around three, I went to her with my grapes. She said no. She said she didn't want them. I put them on the bench anyway. I figured she would eat them later.

"Throw them away if you don't want them," she said.

"If you don't want to eat them, you throw them away. I won't," I said. I knew she wouldn't throw them away. It would have been too great an offence to me and to her nature, her good nature.

Then, she picked them up from the bench and decided to eat them. I smiled. I'd won my way this time. It was beautiful to see her eat them. She would take one big grape and put it in her mouth. The grape would fill her mouth. You could see the bump the grape formed inside her cheek. Then she would take it between her white teeth and crush it. And she would chew it without opening her mouth. And it was done masterly and very lady like. And in doing this she did not look at me but she smiled with the realization that I was watching her.

I hurried up towards the washrooms. Gianni had already changed and was by the Uniconer with two women. Amalia was about to enter the women's washroom. I ran down the walkway to get to her. She was in front of the mirror. I stood there in front of the washroom and watched her setting her hair. I teased her, "Don't forget your lipstick!"

She was smiling and amused and listening to me for a few seconds, setting her hair and then, always smiling, she started to close the washroom door. I blocked the door with my foot. I laughed but then I, suddenly, realized that was not appropriate. I retrieved my foot and let the door close. "Don't forget your lipstick," I shouted.

After I changed, I found her by the punch clock. She had no lipstick on but this I noticed only later. She went to the Uniconer where Gianni was. I followed her. It was then that I remembered about the lipstick. "Why didn't you put your lipstick on?" I said and, then, I added, "Isn't he coming? And then, turning to Gianni himself, "Aren't you coming?"

Without stopping what he was doing, Gianni answered, "I have to teach this lady how to use the Uniconer, Mr. York said. I can't leave now."

"Until what time you have to stay?"

"I don't know. Till seven thirty or eight, maybe."

It was expected Amalia and I would wait for him. We were the only ones left in the factory.

After talking to Gianni, I followed Amalia. But, when she got to the T intersection, she changed her mind and turned back to avoid me. "Amalia!" I shouted. "Stop! Stop for a moment!"

She turned and looked at me, at my frustrated face. "What is it?" she said and walked towards me.

"I want to talk to you," I said. And in my mind I continued saying, *I want to tell you, Amalia, how much I love you, how much I want you, how much I desire you, that you haunt my dreams, that you are my inspiration, that only you can give peace to my warring heart.*

"Come with me!" I said and led the way towards the shipping door. *I want to go where I am alone with you. I want to go where we have fresh air, where we are bathing in the moonlight, and where I can say how my heart aches for you. I love you, Amalia!*

But, on second thought, she turned to me and asked, "Where are we going?"

It was perhaps the euphoria of her consenting to come with me. Pointing with both hands and with a smile on my face, I said, "To get some fresh air."

"You're crazy," she said and turned back. She'd freed herself of that momentary spell I had on her.

I had made light of the situation. I had made a mistake. And I had lost my Amalia with those words.

Amalia went back to the Uniconer and I followed her. She stood by the same box. I was next to her. It was here that I didn't care of anybody present, the two women and Gianni. I was demoralized for I'd missed my chance to talk in private to her.

"Come with me, Amalia. I have to talk to you." But it was too late. That gesture and those words had ruined my chance with Amalia.

I wanted her to respond to me. I touched her arm. She turned to me and said, "Do I have to scream?"

"Are you serious, now?" I said. *You can't hate me. You can't let harm come to me. I'd give my life for you!*

I glanced towards Gianni. He was threading the Uniconer furiously and he looked irritated. "Did you see?" I said. "He looks serious too. He's angry."

"It's all your fault," she said.

I wanted to let her know. "You know, Amalia," I said. "I am like Sir Galahad in search of his Holy Grail. In a poem by Alfred Tennyson, Sir Galahad speaks these words: *I never felt the kiss of love, Nor maiden's hand in mine*. I believe these words apply to me. I am like Sir Galahad."

And off she went. She went back to the punch clock where Mason was. He had a small understanding of English, but, for me, for the way I felt, it was like he did not exist.

She, here too, tried to evade me. She was going back to the Uniconer and I took her by the arm. Her arm quivered under my hand. It seemed I'd touched quick silver and it seemed Amalia liked it and responded to me, not with anger, but with a smile and she stayed still. It seemed that my touching her arm had served again to dominate her, like before when I told her to stop evading me.

She wanted to punch out her card. She went to pick up her card but I got in front of her and I picked up a bunch of cards. She searched for her card among the remaining ones but I had her card. When she realized that, she said, "Give me my card!" I wouldn't.

Seeing I wouldn't give her card, she went to the window, near knitting machine # 1. I went near her. "Do you want you card?" I said. She wanted to move from there and I wouldn't let her pass. She became cross. I let her go.

She sat at the table and I sat to her left on the table. Then she wanted to go out of there. I raised my right leg and put it against the boxes preventing her form getting out. "Let me go!" she said. She once tried to lift my leg. Then, seeing it was futile, her protests against my stubbornness, she sat down again on the chair. She crossed her arms on her chest and made a pouting face. I tried to cheer her up. I fanned the cards in my hands and I said, "Here! Pick your card!"

She didn't move. "We're are not playing games here," she said. "Give me my card!" She was serious. I realized I was bothering her. I didn't want to. I never wanted that. I didn't want her to be angry at me. I loved her.

"I love you, Amalia! I love you so much!" I said and tears were forming in my eyes. I'd never been more sincere. Never a more passionate "I love you!" had been uttered before. This was the first time I'd ever said that to anyone. And all my blood and all my soul were in it. Mason was behind me. He probably understood what I was saying, but I would not have cared if another thousand men had been standing there behind me.

"I'm sorry," she said dryly. "But I don't feel that way." And she trembled and protested with all the force of her body. She looked down when she said that.

"Why don't you go home with me tonight?" I said. "Let me be your escort tonight."

"No! You're crazy. I've always come to work with Gianni. I come to work with him in the morning and I'm going home with him at night. I never found a person kinder and more considerate than Gianni. Gianni is the kindest person I ever met."

"Gianni is a man who can make a woman happy," I said, but what I thought was, *Yes, Amalia, he can make a woman happy, any woman, but not you. I want you for me!*

Mr. York appeared from out of the corridor, where his office was. He was dressed up and was going home. He spoke with Amalia. He was very gallant with pretty girls, that old prick! Then, he asked me about the nylon machine. "It's okay!" I said.

As he went off, going towards the shipping door, Amalia hurried to punch her card. I went to her by the punch clock. "No!" I said. "You punch at 7:30."

"What do you care?

"Wait! Don't punch it now!"

But she punched out anyway. It was 7:17.

With Mr. York gone, Gianni was fast to come from the Uniconer. It was 7:20 and he couldn't punch out his card. Mr. York next day might find out he'd left earlier than he'd been told. He went to Mason. "Mason! Could you do me this favour?

"Sure! Just tell me what I have to do," said Mason. (With the cane he used to work with in his hands and the swaying of his ass, Mason looked like a high-class shepherd.)

"Punch my card out at 7:30," Gianni said and instructed Mason where to punch it.

I remember going home, walking in queue in the corridor. The stairwell was gloomy under the restaurant neon lights, but even gloomier were our hearts, especially mine. In spite of that, in the semi darkness, her face, painted by the uniform, warm light, was enchanting.

We were walking along St. Lawrence St. now. Amalia walked in the middle. I walked to her right. None of us was talking. I looked up at the sky. There was no beautiful sunset tonight. The sky was a gray discolored mass of vastness. But just looking up at the sky was a relief. And the only escape from the unspoken hostility and tension that surrounded me was that gray infinity.

I looked down and I was again surrounded with that same tension. We were about to pass under the railway bridge.

"Well, no one says anything, tonight?" went Gianni cheerfully.

"Look!" I said. "Even the sky is sad because Amalia is going to leave us soon to go back to school."

Amalia laughed but went back to being moody again. I was broken-hearted and it was so evident for anyone to see. She was the only one who could soothe the turmoil in my heart.

On the bus, Gianni and Amalia sat on the last double seat and I sat on the long lateral seat facing theirs. I got up to get off at the Sauve metro station. I said something to Gianni and, then, I turned to Amalia and, in English, I said, "Sometime I can be such a jerk." She smiled but with contempt. I got a glimpse of Gianni. He looked glum. I said goodbye, but both of them did not answer.

SEPTEMBER 9

I woke as usual thinking about Amalia, but this morning my anguish reached a higher pitch. I was starting my shift at the factory at four o'clock in the afternoon. I lingered a little in bed with my eyes wide open. I thought that the first thing I would do was to apologize to her.

At around two, I was at the factory. I couldn't wait. I couldn't stay home with that anguish. I would have two full hours to spend by her.

When I entered the factory, I saw that Paul, Mr. Knight's nephew, was working with Amalia. I had not foreseen that. I said hello. Amalia did not answer me. I passed by and went to put away my lunch bag.

When I came back to the bench, with Paul there, I approached her. "About last night, Amalia, ..." I began to say.

And she attacked me. (This was something else I hadn't foreseen.) "Listen you! I don't want to talk to you. I've told you a hundred times that my boyfriend is jealous and he doesn't want me to talk to anybody. Now, you just leave me alone and don't come here to talk to me."

"Why do you talk to me like that?"

"This is the only way to make you understand."

"All I want is your friendship. You're friends with everybody here at the factory, but I, I alone, can't have your friendship, I, I alone, who craves your friendship more than anybody."

She gave me a wry smile and said, "Yes, you alone!"

Mr. Knight came along the corridor. "Well, Mario! When do you start working?"

"I start at four."

"Did you punch your card?"

"No. I did not."

Then, he changed his boss-like demeanor and, smiling, he said, "When's the wedding, Mario? Take her! Marry her!" and, rubbing the palms of his hands, he added, "And that's done!"

I couldn't but smile at him. "It's not that easy, Mr. Knight." Amalia paid no attention to our conversation.

When Mr. Knight left, Paul came to me and said, "You like Amalia?"

"Yeah," I said and nodded.

"Now I understand what my uncle wanted to say."

"Mr. Knight is a joker," I said.

"Do you love her?" said Paul. Amalia was setting up a box.

"Yes." I looked towards her. "I do," I said. And I was proud to say it. I was smiling but I was holding back my tears.

"And she doesn't love you?"

"Yeah!" I muttered and the smile faded from my lips.

"Then, my friend, you have to leave her alone. If she doesn't love you, you can't force her."

"I don't want to force her," I said.

I was working in the nylon room when one of the women came to tell me that Gianni had boasted at lunchtime that he had already kissed Amalia. Did Amalia kiss Gianni because of what happened the night before, because I bothered her? My heart was in turmoil. I was dejected. I wanted so much for Amalia to be mine. I was desperate. Maybe Gianni could help me. He could help me conquer my Amalia. But first I had to make sure that I wasn't asking the impossible for him. I had to find out for sure if Gianni and Amalia loved each other.

I went to look for Gianni. I found him between the twisters. He was at the inside far end. He was fixing something there. I approached him. "I would like to talk to you, Gianni."

"What is it?" he said from his crouched position.

"Not here. I would like to talk to you in private."

"Wait, then," he said.

I waited there by the twister. Gianni wasn't long with his fixing the twister. He rose, passed by me, and went to the other side of the machine. Maria was on that side of the machine. Gianni went by her, perhaps to tell her that he had fixed that part of the machine. I waited where; but, because I was in so much turmoil, it took me time to notice that they were fooling around. Maria went to get a bobbin from the twister. She wanted to hit him with it or throw it at him. Gianni read her intentions and ran away. He was laughing. Maria went after him. Gianni ran down one of the lanes of the twisters, fast and quick like a gazelle chased by a lion. He turned to his left, squeezed through a narrow space that separated the Uniconer from the twisters, and disappeared. Maria came up the lane and reached where I was. She was pleased with herself because she'd scared him off. And she said aloud, "I'll show you. I'll show you." I wasn't at all amused by their antics. I was rather annoyed by the fact that Gianni was gone. Had he forgot that I wanted to talk to him?

I followed him. I had to squeeze through the narrow opening and I finally found him by the shipping door. He was leaning against the doorframe. I approached him. He was panting hard and still smiling. He was panting so hard that his heartbeat was visible on his chest. Jean was there. He was unloading his truck with the hand loader. He saw Gianni and said, "Hey, there! Pay attention!"

"OK!" nodded Gianni. He could hardly speak, then, turning to me, he said, "What is it, Mario?"

"Catch you breath first. And then we'll talk," I said. I'd envisioned talking to him alone, but this would do. Jean didn't understand Italian.

I watched his heartbeat subside, but another heart, my heart, started to beat faster. It was like Gianni's heart and my heart were riding on a seesaw. Gianni's heart was slowing down as my heart was speeding up.

The pause I had suggested for him helped me too. It gave me time to think.

"I don't know," I began. "If what I am about to ask you, right now, is right. I don't know if I have the right to do it, to ask you about it. I don't know how to phrase it. But I have to know. I want to ask only one question. Do you love Amalia, Gianni?"

Gianni looked at me. "Yes, I love Amalia," he said.

"Are you serious with her?"

"Yes."

He told me yes. I wanted help from him. I had gone for help to him. But how can a man ask another man to forgo his happiness? He'd been sincere and honest in his answers. I could see his earnestness for Amalia. A man can't give up his happiness for another man's happiness.

"That's all, Gianni. This is what I wanted to know. Thanks," I said and I turned and I started to go away.

"I'm sorry, Mario," said Gianni.

"It's nothing. Don't worry!" I said and continued walking away.

I went in the machine room. I began working but I couldn't work. I felt cheated, deceived. I promised myself I was going to tell her off. Now it was about six o'clock and she would soon be going home. I decided I would talk to her now. I stopped working. I couldn't work. I needed to vent my feelings. I went to the bench. She was placing the last checked bobbins in a big box. Paul was there and handing out the bobbins to her. And I started, "Now, you listen to me! This is the last time I am going to speak to you, but you listen to me now!" She stood up and smiled. "You fed me lies. All this time you fed me lies. I was sincere with you but you repaid my sincerity with lies, nothing else but lies. Couldn't you tell me that you loved Gianni? I asked you a thousand times."

She wasn't smiling now. "I didn't want the factory to know."

"You didn't want the factory to know but you knew that I wasn't going to tell anyone. You knew I wasn't going to speak. Why, Amalia? Why did you do that to me? You said you didn't want to hurt me and you couldn't have hurt me worse."

And I went away. My eyes had become wet. I thought that if I was going to stay a little longer, I was going to cry, and a man can't be crying in front of a woman.

SEPTEMBER 10

Although I'd worked till twelve midnight and I'd got home at one o'clock in the morning the night before, the next day I was working from 8:00 AM to 4:00 PM. But I did not feel tired. Full of nervous energy as I was, sleep was the least of my concerns. I got to the factory at 7:45. I said good morning, but only Paul answered me, Amalia did not. I went and punched in my card. Seeing the time it was, I put my lunch bag on the boxes by the punch clock and I went back to the bench. Paul might have been my pretext for my going there, but I really wanted to talk to her.

When I addressed her, without letting me continue, she said, "I thought yesterday was the last day you were going to talk to me?"

I was down in spirits, but her words sort of revived me, gave me strength to fight again, persist. A battle had been lost, but the war was not over yet. I expected her to be mad at me, like the day before. No! She was smiling!

"I tried, Amalia, but I can't," I said. "I did it last night. You saw I didn't talk to you, but I can't keep it up. I have to talk to you, Amalia." I was so desperate that I would've been satisfied even with pity as long as it was coming from her.

I thought of something she would be interested in. "Yesterday," I said. "I talked to Gianni in private. I asked him, 'Do you love, Amalia?' and he said, 'Yes, I do.' And I asked him, 'Are you serious about her? ...' And, as I continued, I looked at her. She was smiling and she was listening eagerly and attentively. She wanted me to talk to her, now!

Before lunch I went to see Amalia. I was trying to convince her to keep her promise to pose for me again. Then, out of the blue, I said, "Who tells me that by marrying Gianni you'll be happy?"

"I'm not going to marry Gianni," she said.

"Do you want to hurt Gianni too, then?"

She did not answer and kept looking down at the bobbin.

I noticed Gianni going into Mr. Knight's office.

Her way of treating me, when she smiled at something that I said that she considered amusing, was a revival to my spirit, gave me hope, and made me defiant.

Mr. Knight called Amalia. She patted her skirt with her hands as to set it. I got in front of her at the bench entrance. "Wait!" I said. "Don't go yet! First promise me, assure me that you're going to be happy with Gianni."

I hoped that by delaying her, by giving her just a few seconds to answer me, she would answer to my advantage. I blocked her way and I even touched that very arm that the night before had quivered under my hand. She laughed, circled around me, and went into Mr. Knight's office. But, with her elusiveness, she left me with an illusion of hope, that perhaps she might still be game. She hadn't answered me but I was happy inside for that elusive hope she'd given me.

And it was in this state of emotions, happy at heart that Gianni found me. I was going out into the corridor from the bench enclosing, when I heard him from inside the corridor.

"Achille!" he called and his voice went from piano to forte when he added, "Do you want to leave her alone, yes or no?" He looked stern. I had never seen him like that.

I remained stunned and then, going towards him, I said, "What's your problem, Gianni?"

Reaching the peak of his voice, he said, "You have to leave her alone, you understand?"

"Easy, easy," I said. "You don't need to yell. I'm right here." I was trying to avoid a scene.

"Yesterday you came to me to find out, and I told you. Before you didn't know, but now you do."

"So what? I didn't promise you anything. The pursuit is open to everyone."

"Yesterday you came here at two o'clock to stay with her, and you talked to her until four o'clock when you started to work."

"What four o'clock? I started to work at three o'clock!" I grimaced.

"And the same thing this morning. Before you didn't know, but now you know. You have to stop bothering her! Just go and do your work, that's all!"

While Gianni talked, I gave a glance towards Mr. Knight's office. Amalia was by the door. She was about to come and then retreated inside. At that, I right away thought that Amalia's going into Mr. Knight's office had been Gianni's pretext so he could talk to me alone in the corridor and tell me off.

"You have to stop," continued Gianni and he looked threatening but he didn't threaten. I was waiting for that but he didn't seem to have found the right words.

"You don't scare anybody, Gianni," I finally said, shaking my head. But then I thought, *What kind of people were Gianni and his family? Were they like those peasants my mother used to tell me about? "Those days, they would stab each other to death over a woman!"*

While I was thinking this, Gianni said, "Neither do you!" From his answer, I could tell that this guy did not stab others for love.

I tried to reason with him. "Why is this your business? It's up to Amalia. She decides."

"She has decided. She doesn't want to talk to you. She told me. It's you who comes here to talk to her." Gianni was calmer now. "Now, you have to go away from here and leave her in peace."

Then he went away leaving me in disorientation and distress. I left the corridor to go back to the machine room and it was like someone had been blocking my view with a blanket.

It was noon. By now the whole factory, meaning the women and Mason, knew about my quarrel with Gianni over Amalia. Mina had been in Mr. Knight's office and she had been listening to what we had been saying.

I went to the restaurant to buy a drink. When I came back to the knitting machine area, where I ate lunch, I saw that the women had not gone to eat their lunches at the shipping door, where Amalia and Gianni were having lunch. The women had always had their lunch at the shipping door. I realized they'd done this for me. They had taken my side against Amalia and Gianni. Mia wanted me to sit next to them. But I didn't. I sat on my high box opposite them.

Sonia came and joined us later. I don't know how much she knew about my story with Amalia, but she seemed sincere when she asked me, "Where is Amalia, Mario?"

I didn't want to answer her at first, and then I said with a smile on my face, "Amalia is lost!" Alas, it was so true! Seeing Sonia's puzzled face, I took control of my emotions and, with a straight face this time, I said, "She's over there, by the shipping door."

6D. My Romantic Pursuit Anita

WHERE ARE YOU?

Peace I couldn't find
with you in my mind.
A love night with you made me care.
I came to you but you weren't there.

Do you prefer me or a biker
who has never loved anybody?
I want you to be my partner.
You can't have me and another?

Why are you running this way and that?
Where are you? What are you doing?
I'll love you as no one ever has.
For now, come and sit on my lap!

My story with my romantic pursuit of **Anita** took place in 1970, during the first 12 days of September, **after Secondary 5**, when I was 19, just before I went to college.

DAY 1 (Tuesday, Sept. 1)
The first time I saw Anita, her first day of work at the mail services factory, in the long skirt and the black hair, I thought she was Italian. Clara's comment about her skirt was, "Long, yes; but, not that long!"

She wasn't my inspiration girl. So, when Jean, the truck driver, started flirting with her, it didn't bother me. I wasn't jealous, as I had been with the girl Anita replaced.

At break time, she wanted to go to the canteen truck through the big garage door. You couldn't do that. After, as she was waiting for her turn, she spoke to Chantal.

At lunchtime, she and Chantal were talking with Jean. Jean mentioned something about taking pills. Female secrets? And, then, for a moment, for the first time, the pleasing thought of being her boyfriend came to me. I thought of sharing her female secrets.

At lunchtime, she was sitting with Chantal, not too far away from the rest of us, at the receiving doors. They were talking. Then, she started to speak English with Paula. I found out, from her talking with Paula, that she was Spanish. Chantal had to go and answer a phone call. She made Paula notice Chantal's mayonnaise sandwich. She spoke of the Spanish tortilla. She showed Paula her photo album. I approached Paula and had a look too. I was interested in the poems at the end of the album.

"I write English as I speak it," she said.

I took the album and read the poem 'Science In Love'. I was very enthusiastic about it. I brought it to the attention of Paula. As Paula and Clara couldn't read English, I translated part it for them. However, I made several errors, because I hadn't understood what the poem was about.

"What is it? It's the tongue, isn't it?" I asked her at the end of lunch. She did not answer. I also asked her what she meant by a certain phrase about her mother. And I asked for a copy of the poem I had been reading.

At a certain moment when Paula was looking at the poems in the photo album, the idea that my girlfriend was a poet was a wonderful thought. I knew very few, if any, could appreciate her poetry. For example, Paula wouldn't or couldn't.

During the afternoon break, they were sitting outside. Chantal was writing. I thought it was for herself. She, Anita, never turned her head once. Jean was there too. When she was finished, Chantal gave me a copy of the poem. Then Jean asked to read it. Chantal asked if I was going to translate it into English.

"Maybe," I said.

On the way home, on the bus, she was sitting with her legs crossed. She was glancing at me. I was too proud to care. I had been drawing Louiselle that day. Anyway, she was a pleasing sight: the thick thighs, the pursed lips, the makeup, and the black hair. She had about her an air of sophistication, while I must've had an air of naiveté.

That night, I set myself to work, and with my nephew's help at first, I translated the poem, and I understood its meaning. The poem was about her feelings during lovemaking.

DAY 2 (Wednesday, Sept. 2)

In the morning I found them by the receiving door. I said good morning. I said it mainly for her but only the old woman answered. I sat down and I took the photo album from her. She continued talking in French. I looked for the words I couldn't identify in Chantal's handwriting.

At break time, I showed my English translation to Paula. The blond girl and Richard read it too. I urged Anita to publish her poems. She offered to give me her album after work, so I could read the rest of her poems.

At four thirty, when I got the album from her, I explained when I was going to bring it back. Outside, I asked her, "How long is it you've been writing poetry?" And we made our way to the bus stop together.

I asked her about how long she was in Canada, if she always went to French school, and if she read and wrote Spanish. She was giving me some tips about some Italian and Spanish words. "Where did you learn those Italian words?" She told me about her father making five hundred dollars a week. "I'm making one tenth of your father's pay," I said.

When we got on the bus, she stood next to me. She said she couldn't think of me being English as I had black hair. I said that Richard, who was standing beside us, was English-speaking. "I know," she said. She meant he was irrelevant. This gave me some victory points. She asked me how long I'd lived in Canada. I asked her where she lived. We found out that we lived within walking distance to each other. She made me understand that she shared a flat with a family of five children, and the annoyance the children gave her, and her girlfriend, and throwing dishes at her husband, when she had to eat, "I want this. I want that. Letting it fall on the floor."

At the metro station stop, she decided to take the metro too. In the station I was directing her.

At the Fleury bus stop, some remarks about her jet black hair. She asked me if I liked red hair. She didn't. She wanted to die her hair blonde.

On the bus she sat on the side front seat. I sat next to her. A woman looked at us. She talked about the people she lived with. What do you do after supper in the evening? Her question was so unexpected. I wanted to ask her out. To do that, I wanted to get off with her at the same bus stop, but she might've found that odd, and so I didn't.

Back home, my brother and his family from Belgium were visiting. Gianmarco, my childhood friend from Italy, was there too. I showed the photo album to my folks. I wondered at how she could have written such things. My brother said, "They're not like you and me. Sex is not such a taboo to them as it is to us. They start when they're very young."

DAY 3 (Thursday, Sept. 3)

Next morning, it was pleasantly surprised that, while I was sitting in the Cremazie bus, I saw her advancing in the bus. She had taken the subway. She wore pants. I gave her my seat. She was radiant. She complained she was late. She told me her girlfriend had played a trick on her, at three o'clock in the morning. I was standing in front of her. I gave her the publisher's address. "It's a fine day, today," she said, not knowing what to say.

We got off the bus and crossed the bridge to get on the other side of the highway. I asked her if she'd gone out the night before. Then, I asked her if she'd like to go out with me tonight.

"Okay!" she said. "I'll give you my address after work."

We agreed to go out at around seven thirty. I asked her where she'd like to go. She said anything I decided was okay with her. "A movie?" I said.

And we got to the factory, satisfied, fulfilled. This I could surely say of myself, and of her too, I guessed. We were going to be together at night.

I said that we were going to be a little late. As we came into the lobby, she made me notice the clock on the wall. It was past eight by two or three minutes. I said, "Morning!" I had seen George. He and Jean answered me. I punched my card, went to the washroom, and went to work. And she did the same.

As soon as I got a breather, I continued wondering, as before, at how easy it had been to ask her out. She was there, sitting at her machine, working. And I got self-conscious again. I straightened my body. She was not working close to me and her back was turned away from me most of the time.

I once passed in front of her and said, "Getting tired?" She smiled. I worked with enthusiasm. I was enthusiastic even in the way I related to George and Joe.

Then a doubt took possession of me. What if she changed her mind? In the evening I would know for sure.

Not much happened during the entire working day, except at the 3:15 break. I offered her my grapes, as I had done with the others. It was actually her I cared about. She said no. "Why?" I said. "Because I don't like grapes," she said. That worried me. I spent an anxious hour, but, at four thirty, after having punched my card, she was waiting for me outside.

She gave me her address and we agreed again on the time. I was going to pick her up. At the bus stop, she talked with the Ukrainian girl and her friend, the one who was going to college.

On the bus, she showed me a poem she'd been writing during the day. I marveled at how fast she wrote poems.

In the subway, we met Jean, and she talked with him most of the time. I was relieved that he wasn't getting off at the same station as us. On leaving he said to me, "Good night. Don't do anything that I wouldn't do." I thought about what I had to do to get ready.

I got home and washed my hair in all haste and I neglected my little niece visiting from Belgium.

By a quarter to eight I was at her place. I first rang downstairs. Then, getting no answer, I went up the stairs and knocked at the door. She was in shorts. She introduced me to the kids and Pierrette. After several bids of 'enjoy yourself', we left. We were outside, when Pierrette called from the balcony reminding her that she'd forgotten the 'shield'. She went back to get it. I asked Anita what Pierrette meant. She told me that by 'shield' she meant her purse. I told her we would go to Expo 67 instead of going to see a movie. We crossed the street to get to the bus stop. I wanted to pay for her fare too, but she didn't let me.

On the bus, we sat in the back. She made me see that she was in Spanish attire. "Oh, yes!" I said. She was wearing a lot of mascara. We'd both dressed up: she in her Spanish attire and I in my suit, a suit I was using for the second time. There were other couples on the bus. We talked and, without noticing it, we had arrived at the metro station.

In the subway we talked about how many children a family should have. "On Monday morning I am glad I am going back to work," she said. At Berri-de-Montegny we switched to the Longueuil line. "How do you say 'God bless you' in French?" I said. At the end of the line, when already on Expo 67 grounds, we had to get off. We looked for the events board. "You're like me," she said. "You don't know all the words in French and I don't know all the words in English." We held hands. We had to go to the other side of the St. Lawrence Bridge to get to the events board. We seemed to be late for all the shows. We noticed the small souvenir shops. We did some window-shopping.

We crossed the bridge back. I took her on the monorail even though she was sort of protesting. On the monorail train, we got to do a tour of the different pavilions. I had my arm around her.

"Give me a kiss!" I said. She offered herself spontaneously.

After kissing, she said, "I didn't know I was going to fall in love with an Italian."

I took out my handkerchief and wiped her lipstick off my lips. "I like your lips but I don't like the taste of your lipstick," I said. And I did a most unpardonable thing. **I tried to wipe her lipstick off her lips too!** She flinched.

We continued with the tour of the pavilions. At one time, we went through the US pavilion. I held her face in my hands. I looked into her eyes. She looked into mine. This was quite a woman! I was so lucky!

I caressed her bare arms. Her arms were cold to the touch, even though her hands were warmer than mine. I asked her again if she was cold. I took off my jacket and put it around her shoulders.

It was the end of the ride. The monorail train stopped. We lingered on. An attendant came and pressed us to get off. I was aroused. I wasn't wearing my jacket; so I couldn't hide my erection. And, to make things worse, as we were getting off, I banged my head against an overhang.

We came down the platform, and I saw the main events board in Place des Nations, right there, in front of us. We saw that there was nothing on. All shows were over or about to end. It was pretty late now. Pondering where to go, we walked into some remote and isolated corner of the fair.

We walked on some bridge. We were all alone. I was telling her about my resolutions for the future. I emphasized how much I loved drawing, painting, and that I wanted to write.

"It's life I want to understand. It's the mysteries of life that stir me, enthrall me, entice me, and twist me in their marvelous pleasures," I said.

We were descending the stairs, when I realized that what I was telling her might disillusion her. Did she count on me working and supporting her? She told me about her family. Her older sister lived in Canada; but her younger sister lived in Spain with her mother.

"What do you want in life?" I said.

"Not money. I hate money," she said.

"Do you want to get married?"

"My older sister says, 'I'm twenty three. This is not the time. I want to enjoy my life now that I am young.'"

We came to the entrance of a pavilion. I wanted to go in. It was closed. We walked on and came to the edge of the water of Notre Dame Island. I invited her to sit on the bench. She didn't want. Then, when she saw that, not too far from us, some people were also sitting on a bench, she sat down. She crossed her legs and put her purse in her lap.

When we kissed, she gave herself abundantly, but not with passion. She kept her arms on her purse. But, it was now that I finally tasted the pleasure of our kiss. I tasted her moist lips and her hot mouth. I was aroused.

I wanted to try with her a breath kiss, where one breathes through the mouth of the other. "Ugh, I don't like it," she said.

I took her face in my hands, her mascaraed face, kissing her on the cheeks, at the corner of her mouth, and on her pursed lips.

"Look at me!" I said.

"I look at you, so what?"

"You'll see!" I said. I slipped my hand, my very cold hand, inside her dress and I touched the nipple of one of her breasts, and then the other. And I felt the warmth of her chest and the pounding of her heart.

She let me touch her without protesting until I stroked her thigh. "I'm Spanish!" she said.

I knew! And I gathered that to her that meant 'hard-headed'. But to me it meant 'hot'.

"Perhaps you would think bad of me. I don't want to think bad of me," she said.

I unbuttoned her blouse. At first she let me do it and then she said, "No. Stop!"

"Okay. As you wish."

"I'm not one of those girls," she said.

"It's the whole of you that counts, not ten seconds of pleasure," I said. "I hope you give me a chance to know me." I stroked her thighs. "Please, uncross your legs."

"No! I know what you want to do."

"No, I assure you. How do you want me to show my love for you?"

Unmoved soul! But I realized what a chance I had. I realized how close I was to those legs and how close I was to stroking those thighs.

I looked at the wayward water of the river. I persisted. "Get on my lap," I said.

"No! I know what you want to do."

"Sit on my lap, please. Okay, get up."

"What do you want to do? Do we go home?"

"No! Your purse, your shield, put it beside you."

"Why?" she said.

"Because I want to hold you in my arms."

I took her purse and put it beside her, but she put it right back into her lap.

"If I let you have me the first time we go out, what will you think of me?"

DAY 4 (Friday, Sept. 4)
In the morning I saw her on the bus. I waited for her at the metro station. She greeted me as if nothing had happened between us the night before. It was a day of drudgery. In the evening she told me that she couldn't go out because she'd to visit her grandmother who'd come from Spain. We made an appointment for two o'clock next day. When we parted, I said, "Don't I get a kiss?" *You promised me that the next time we went out, we would make love.*

DAY 5 (Saturday, Sept. 5)
When I went to her place at around two thirty next day, I didn't find her there. Pierrette told me she'd gone out at eleven. I went back at around five o'clock. She came out with a small child at her hand. She was going to the store. She told me the child was her niece, but that did not match what she'd told me about her sister. At the store I bought a pinwheel for little Line, the child. On the way back I carried the child in my arms. In front of her house, I said, "Here's your niece." And I gave her my phone number.

DAY 6 (Sunday, Sept. 6)
Sunday morning I felt the emptiness of the house after my brother and his family had left the night before. I was waiting for a phone call from Anita. My friend Tony made my kid brother drive his car. My friend Dick and I went to her place. It was raining. Pierrette told me that Anita had gone out at six. She was a little vexed at me for my showing up there.

DAY 7 (Monday, Sept. 7)
Early on Labor Day morning, Tony, Frank, and I had an excursion on St. Gregoire Mountain. I was in a hurry to get back. I wanted to go and see her. Back in town, I didn't want Tony to drive in front of her house. Later, I passed in front of her house. I saw a woman cleaning a window. I didn't call on her.

DAY 8 (Tuesday, Sept. 8)
On Tuesday, we didn't talk all day. It was a day of mortification. I waited for her at the bus stop.

I had brought back her album, a French-English dictionary, and a poem I had written about her on Monday night.

The bus was packed. I was standing next to her. I read my poem to her.

"That's cute," she said.

I wanted her to get off with me at the Cremazie subway station.

First, she said she was going to her uncle's. Then, she said, "I'm going with *madame*." She meant the old lady sitting in front of us.

"Do you want to go out with me?"

"I don't know. When I look at somebody, I know. I like to be alone."

"I know. You're a poet."

"Me and my poetry!" she said

"Let's get off at the next stop."

"No!" she said. "Oh, that's Jean!" And she turned to talk to Jean.

At home I reflected about caring for her. *When an old lady or a fool pleases you more than I do, then, go, by all means. You ruined my peace. Perhaps it is better this way now that I am going back to school. My best wishes to you and your poetry.*

DAY 9 (Wednesday, Sept. 9)
I waited for her at the bus stop. In the morning, before we started to work, she was sitting with Jean. *I've had a sleepless night because of her and she talks with Jean.*

She readily posed for me at lunch and at the 3:15 break. The fact that I drew her changed nothing. She said she was not leaving at the usual time tonight because she was working overtime.

"*Ciao, ciao, allora!*" I said.

I'd never seen her work overtime, before!

DAY 10 (Thursday, Sept. 10)
I went to Dawson College for my registration.

DAY 11 (Friday, Sept. 11)
It was my last day at the mail services factory.

At the break, I said, "Hello!"

"Hi!" she said.

DAY 12 (Saturday, Sept. 12)
In the afternoon, I went to her house. I saw the little boy, Jean, in front of her house.

"Jean. Is Anita there?" I said.

"Yes," he said.

"Tell her Mario's here. I'm Mario." The kid snickered, as his mother appeared.

"Mom, there's a man here who..." Jean started to say.

"I told you that Anita is not here! She can't go out!" she said and she shut the door.

"Jean. Is Anita there? Yes or no?" I said.

"No. She's not here."

I lingered there and then I said, "Come on. Come with me. Let's go to the store. I'll buy you something." Jean sneered at the suggestion. I waited. He was not coming and I asked again, "Is she or is she not there?"

"No."

"Tell me the truth. She's there, right?"

"Yes."

"She's there but they say she isn't, right?"

"Yes. Mother doesn't want her to go out with you," he said.

"Mother? It's not her that decides. She's not Anita's mother. Anita shares just room and board here." Then, I changed my tone and said, "I want to talk to her. Wait for me here! I'm going to the store to buy a pen and paper. I'm going to write a massage for her and you're going to bring it to her. All right?" The boy nodded. I was going when the door opened.

"Is he still there? asked Pierrette. Anita was behind her.

"I'm still here," I said.

"What do you want?" said Anita. "I can't go out with you. I told you."

I don't want to go out," I said. It's not that. I came here to see if you had nothing special to do. I want you to pose for me."

"No! I have to go out. I can't! ... I'm getting married. I don't have time to ..."

"Married? So soon? Come on. You're lying?"

"No. It's true!" said Pierrette. "She has a kid. It's the guy she had the child with. He's going to marry her now."

"A child?" I exclaimed. Then, looking at Anita, I said, "Come with me. I want to talk to you, to tell you something."

"Talk. Talk. I don't have anything to say to you. I don't have time for you."

"Make time." I looked at my watch. "Just five minutes."

The man of the house came out onto the balcony. "Get inside, you," he told his son. Then, speaking to me, he declared, "She doesn't want to go out, okay?"

I said to Anita, "Come with me. I want to talk to you."

I don't have the time," she said. Then, looking towards the man, she said something and she went inside.

"What did she say?" I asked the man. "Is she coming out?"

"No!"

"What did she say?"

"She said, 'See you on Monday'."

"Monday? I'm not working on Monday. I'm finished."

"Ah, you're finished?"

"I used to work where she worked. But I'm going back to school now. I'm starting on Monday."

"You know, she's just seventeen and a half. She'll be eighteen in November, two months from now. You know, I don't want anybody here. I don't want her to bring guys here." He made a gesture with both hands. "If she goes out, okay! Because, you know, it's every goddamn night. A goddamn guy every fucken night! Yesterday night another guy was here."

"That was me. I was here yesterday night and your wife told me that she'd gone out."

Ah, I don't think it was you. Anyway, as I was saying, yesterday night a guy was here, today it's you, and tomorrow it's another! She never goes out with the same guy. She changes every night. You know, it's me who has charge of her. I could send her to prison this very minute, you know."

"You say you're have charge of her. How come? Doesn't she have a father?"

"Yes, she has. But he don't want her, you see? Her father don't want her. They don't want her."

"But her father came to pick her up yesterday night, your wife told me, when I was here yesterday night."

"Yes, but that's rare. They don't want her. She was given to me. It was when she lived with her mother right here next door. It was then when they said, 'Do you want to take her?' I said, 'All right, as long as she goes to work.' And she went to work. But it's always the same goddamn thing. She never changes."

"But is it true that she has a child? A kid? Does she really have a kid?"

"Yes! It's fourteen or fifteen months old. She had given it away after the sixth or seventh day." The man made a gesture of distaste. "She was in a house where they put children in, you know."

"Orphanage."

"Here you can take them later if you want."

"You know, it's funny now looking back. She used to talk about five children and how they used to irritate and annoy her. The only time I went out with her. I brought her to Man and His World. We were talking about how many children a family should have. I believing, poor fool, I knew more. I decided for three and we settled with that. At another time, wanting her to meet a little niece of mine, I said, 'I know you don't like children, but you'll like this one.' Because I was thinking of the way she'd spoken of your children. 'Oh, but I do like children," she said. And her answer somewhat surprised me, but now I know it shouldn't have."

"Well, what can you do!" There was some shouting coming from inside. The man turned and said, "You go in the living room!"

"Do you want to tell her, please, if she wants to come out just for a moment. I don't want anything from her. I just want to explain a few things to her."

"Anita, the guy only wants to talk to you. Listen, it's your business, but..."

And she came out on the balcony, and the man went in. "What do you want?" she said.

"Come, come with me. Let's take a walk. I can't talk here."

"What do you want to tell me? Talk here."

"Okay. Come down at least." And she came down. "You look so much prettier with no mascara and make up on," I said. She pouted. "Not like when you went out with me. You were covered with makeup, eyes and face and all, as to protect yourself against me."

"What is it you want from me?" she said.

"Why didn't you tell me before that you were getting married?"

"He only asked me last week. I only knew a week ago. I'm getting married in two months. I already told them at work, to the forelady, that soon I was going to leave work. I'm not going to work. I'm going to take care of my child."

"Is he a Canadian or a Spaniard like you?"

"A Spaniard."

"You told me so many lies."

"Yes."

"Why didn't you tell me before?"

"Because I didn't know you."

"And you know me now?"

"Yes! No!" She didn't want to commit to yes or no.

"I could've helped you, even now. I'm not like other guys. I'm different."

"When you asked me if loved you, I told you."

"I never asked you such a thing!" I said.

"I told you that if I liked someone, it was me who went for him. It is you who has insisted, coming so many times to look for me when I clearly showed you that I wasn't interested in you."

"Do you really have a child?"

"Yes, Achille."

"Is it the little girl you were with, on Saturday, a week ago, when I came looking for you and you were going to the store?"

"Yes, Achille."

"Then it was your child I was holding in my arms?"

"Yes, Achille."

"And you told me it was your niece. But that couldn't be because none of your two sisters is married. But how was I, poor fool, to know? Today I wanted to bring you to my place to draw your picture, the picture you wanted, remember? I thought I wanted to tell you, 'You are a poet, yes, but you don't know the value of life'. But, I didn't know that you had given life. So long, Anita. Take care of yourself. Be happy in your life."

7A. My Friend Jenny

I HAD NO IDEA

She walks quietly into the classroom.
She is barefoot and without socks.
She joins us at the tables end.
She sits in the teacher's chair.

Her eyes that come haunting like stars,
They reflect light when she looks up.
Those lips! Those sinuous lips!
They extend and stretch as she smiles.

How? How on earth?
How enchanting! How incredible!
I need a better look with my glasses on.
I had no idea this beauty was in my class!

I was **in college** when I met Jenny.

Jenny, sweet her name, just to hear it, read it scribbled on the toilet wall, evoking images and memories dear to me, and nourishing my mind and body.

Not remembering your name, but remembering my touching you. My gesture was bold and daring. Oh, to gently and softly touch your shoulder! How aflutter was my breast at the touch of you!

I am thankful to my Jenny. My joyless heart falls in love with your beauty. Again! Again! Your eyes are slightly brushed with mascara, a celestial color, to heighten their heavenly beauty.

WHO IS JENNY?

"Who is Jenny?" I asked.

"I don't know," said Fanny. "She's supposed to give her presentation with us, but she's absent."

And next class I learned who Jenny was.

It was the bare-footed girl, sitting at the presentation desk, by the teacher, like a pet. She was there, protected and safe, by the motherly wings of *Monsieur Charet*.

I was sitting very close by her left. She was looking at Fanny or me. I hoped it was at me.

Your lips, Jenny, supple and sweet, the bliss that to a kiss they must give! I am trying to imagine, as they curve and surge, how they would feel, warm and wet and pressing softly against my lips.

When she spoke, her voice sounded, to me, melodious. Such a delicate and sweet sensation! And that musical timbre, so peculiar to you! Ah, when hearing it for the first time and forever echoing in my brain! And here it went, bare and naked, caressing and soothing, as it reached the vibrating drums of my ears. I want you to say my name in a loop. "Hi, Achille!" "Hi, Achille!" "Hi, Achille!" …

Your lips, so well-formed and full and soft! The nose, so proportioned and perfect and flawless!

"You made my nose too big, I think," she said.

"I wanted to give you my nose," I said.

Those lovely eyes, accentuated by long eyelashes to heighten their beauty! Jenny, your eyes are the soothing oasis in the desert, the luxurious palace in the slum, and the bright sky in the night.

Trying to imagine naked you! Oh, to die for! Those beautiful breasts, that love triangle, and those buttocks I want to spank like you do!

Coming closer and touching me. Me? Oh, let me cry out, let me jump up, and let me kneel down to The One who allows for the existence of such a wonder!

"Hi, Achille!" Emerging like the sun shining on the morning dew! What a vision! Spring has come with you. Ouch, that boldness! How could you, to me a rare flower in a thousand fields in bloom, call me a friend? Tell me! No! Don't! How can I? What? How could you? And once you dared. You would repeat my name, once again, and again, as an echo, and coming like delicate rain, soft snow, and pattering hail. Say my name! Say my name!

"I could understand that," another voice insinuates in my mind.

That sad time when I saw you with your boyfriend, sitting with him on the stairs of the Selby campus, and you had your slender, slim arm around his. So sweet! So sweet!

Usurper! Plunderer of my dreams! That's Jenny!

Or, is it I the usurper, the serpent crawling under her skirt, as she's sitting on the floor, and biting her love triangle?

But, maybe, you're the serpent's instrument, like the time you said, "Do you want to take a bite from my apple?" Before you had time to think, I was biting, biting as much I could. You hand was unsteady. And I was trying to avoid your fingers with my teeth but not with my lips. I took a chunk of apple but I smeared the rest of the apple with my saliva. Are you going to eat my saliva, now? "Thanks!" I said, chewing your sweet fruit. Ah, the bite into that apple was epic! Let's do it a thousand times more. I accept! I accept! Thank you, beautiful Jenny!

Sitting in the teacher's office, I was talking to Jenny. I had made a foolish remark during her presentation about her belief in reincarnation. "I think that is an infantile belief," I said, but Lily, coming to her rescue, said, "That's what **you** believe. Show some respect!"

Talking to Jenny was delightful. My treasure, bending forward and raising her head, with her hair behind her ear and with the side of her face to me, sat on the table and gave all of her attention to me.

"Yes, Achille," she said.

I finally answered, "As I was saying, Jenny, I'm sorry if I hurt your feeling when, in class, I said that to believe in reincarnation is childish."

It was in **March** and Jenny aroused me!

WHO IS CRYING?
O Jenny, hopeless and impossible, unattainable and fleeting, light and diaphanous, rosy and white in the nebulous mists of my dreams!

O Jenny, I want to have you just for myself; but, you were born for many; you're part of the wind.

One May day, Jenny was crying by my locker and a guy was consoling her. No girl has ever cried for me, Jenny!

I went to the Humanities class at the Viger campus. The teacher did not show up. I was going down, looking from the top of the staircase, from the third floor, and a group of students passed by behind me. Was that Jenny?

I took ten minutes by bus to get back to the Selby campus. I was lost in a moment of reverie, when all things are futile and wonderful at the same time, when a dream is about to fall apart to give rise to renewed hope. I was going to the library. Just as I turned the corner, I heard the sound of a voice and I saw a girl and a boy by my locker. The girl was facing my way. I looked at her face. Jenny! She was crying! I wondered why. You tell me? You tell me! Why?

Walking slow, looking and not looking, just enough to be able to walk, my mind was everywhere and nowhere, wondering, wondering about her. Why was **this girl** crying for her boyfriend?

"You don't have to wait for me," she sobbed softly.

And, yes, I was ready to concede to her now, "It's okay to believe in reincarnation, Jenny!"

WHO'S JOHN?

It was a great surprise to see her, on that **November** night. I had been thinking about her.

At the end of my German class, I was coming from the Richelieu campus with Vicky, to whom I had asked if she wanted to come and watch *La Vraie Nature de Bernadette*. Anyway, I had to go to the Selby library to find a book by Sartre. It was part of *Le programme d'echanges*.

In the library, I found *L'existentialisme* by Sartre and I was looking for his biography in the encyclopedia section when this girl approaches me at the counter and said, "Hi!"

"Hi, Jenny!" I said, without hesitation, remembering the name of my ideal girl.

"Let me see if I remember your name. Achille! Is that it?"

"Yeah!" Surely, you must be kidding, Jenny, after all those memorable, sweet 'Hi, Achille!' last year.

She worked, didn't go to university, needed money, and was taking a course at Dawson.

Her mustached, unrecognizable ex-boyfriend passed by with a group and said to her, "Is that John?"

"Who's John?" I said.

"Just a guy who looks like you. He's got a beard like you," she said.

He was going downstairs to the cafetaria, leaving to me my precious Jenny. Ah, to just look in her eyes!

Then she left me when she saw a guy pass by in the corridor outside the library. She excused herself and was about to go to him, when a guy got in front of her and stopped her. I found out later he was another one of her friends.

Later, the guy who had passed by joined us too. I had seen this guy around. He was very jumpy. Maybe he was high. He asked her why she had not visited him.

"I couldn't find the place," she said.

He wanted to go. She offered to give him 50 cents to have him stay. I understood they were good friends. Oh, Jenny! What about me? When she went to get the money, she looked back at me, my eyes, my shortsighted eyes.

In the meantime, this second guy found me a book on existentialism at the counter. I should have offered to pay his meal before Jenny. He was kind. I could see why she was friends with him.

She came back and, when she got in front of us, she announced her presence by slapping, at the same time, both of her blue-jeaned, gorgeous buttocks.

I reminded her of when she was crying in front of ex-boyfriend. "Yes, those eyes were crying," I said.

"Oh, it couldn't be, Achille," she said.

"It wasn't a bad sight, anyway. A girl crying for a guy."

When all three of them left, she said, "It was good to see you, Achille."

"And you. Not just good. Very, very good." Those smiling lips I had fantasized about so many times!

"I'll see you, Achille, around seven? Next Monday?" she said.

"I don't know if I can," I said.

"Anyway, take care, Achille!"

"Yeah. You too."

She was going downstairs to the cafeteria with her two boyfriends. And, with Sartre's book in my hands, I was left to muse about how enchanting she was. *Yes, Jenny, I'll be here on Monday.*

When I went downstairs, I saw them coming out of the cafeteria. I changed my route to preserve the enchantment I'd had with her. When going to take my 90 bus on St. James, I thought, *If I were a prince, Jenny, I would not hesitate a moment to court you. How can people look at you and not worship you? O Jenny! My friend! My love!*

7B. My Friend Fanny

LOVABLE FRIEND

How sweet you are, Fanny,
with every action of yours.
A nudge to draw my attention,
to free me from what's worrying me
and you succeed, you perk me up!

A pretended frown,
a look into my eyes,
and as your smile forms,
you tame me, my will,
and make me wiser.

I never met a lovelier girl!
This is what I wanted to tell.
I am thrilled when I see you!
Aw, come on, now, Achille!
O lovable, married Fanny,
Come! Let's cuddle up!

IN JUNE
I was in college at the time. I went to bring back the
tape recorder. A windy day in June, I was on St.
Catherine Street and coming from Dawson College. I
was in my coffee windbreaker and coffee pants.
When I was about to enter Westmount Square, a girl,
with a most wonderful body, shiny in her beautiful
legs, detached from the group of girls she was with,
hurrying ahead past the girls, and came rushing
towards me. I instantly recognized her. It was **Fanny**!
The wind was blowing her super miniskirt and

exposing more of her gorgeous legs. She was coming towards me, arm outstretched, and hand extended.

"*Allô! Bonjour! Ça va?*"

"*Oui, et toi?*"

I don't remember if I said anything more, too dumbfounded at seeing her, at the unexpected sight of her. I was so ecstatic at seeing her. She shook my hand and leaned forward for a kiss. That was unexpected too. I moved in with my beard and kissed the side of her mouth, her wet moist mouth, that so many times I saw move and speak!

"How are you?" she said.

Too incredulous still to believe what I was seeing, "Astounded!" I said at last.

"Aw, come on, Achille!" she said. I loved to hear her say my name. "I feel high because I just had a drink."

"Where are you going?"

"Now I'm to have lunch. I'm with these girls. We're going to a restaurant. I'm with that girl over there."

"You didn't call me up once," I said, pointing at her with my finger.

"I know. I didn't have time. Listen. I'm in group therapy. We're just coming from the hospital."

"What is that? What is it? Work?"

"Now I don't have the time. I'll call you up and explain all to you. Now me and the girls are going to the restaurant to have lunch."

"The psychologist?"

"I'm only a patient now. I'll call you up and I'll explain all to you."

"Okay, okay!" I touched and caressed her face, that pretty spectacled face. I did it twice, to make sure that it was she, that it hadn't been a mistake. We did a hasty handshake and off my girl, my married girl, went, to be caressed by the wind in her super miniskirt. I wished I had been the wind touching, caressing, and kissing her all over. I turned around and opened the spring-powered door still dumbfounded. She was really there, in her super miniskirt, all nice and caring and sweet to me! Fanny! Fanny!

I remember the first time I saw Fanny. She was giving her character presentation. She wore a white skirt. She was sitting on the chair and I was sitting on the carpet. The view I had of her beautiful thighs!

IN SEPTEMBER
At the beginning of the school year, in September, I had an appointment with Fanny in the Selby caf at 9:30. Later, we went and had lunch in the Jacques Cartier Park. I said to her, "Before I used to ask God forgiveness for masturbating, now I thank Him for it."

IN MARCH
One March day, I was in the Selby cafeteria with her, after the English class, talking of Salinger, futile things, and about her husband returning home next day. I felt like a miracle maker. She was so close and receptive! The air was ripe with sexual liberation. I decided to communicate to the fullest with her.

"Fanny," I said. "It's rather hard for me to tell you and I don't know how you're going to take it; but, during the past weekend, I masturbated two or three times thinking about you." Her mouth got wide open. "I hope you don't feel offended," I added.

"On the contrary, Achille," she said, her eyes brightening. "It is an honor you do me. Only you are much too much for me, I'm at a loss with you. It is difficult for me, the change, what's happening."

"What do you mean?"

"I mean here comes along this man with more experience than me, waltzing me and my life along in my thoughts and ideas."

7C. My Friend Elena

ONE AND ALL

In this immense search,
In this intense want,
Pulled by all sides,
This girl is beautiful,
That other is gorgeous.

I attach myself to all,
Every one that offers hope,
I adore and cherish each one.
I see the sublime
In one and all.

I sway and waver,
Attracted here and there,
I give all of myself,
And I'm bound to fail
In what I'm looking for.

And then the pain of delusion,
I find out it was only an illusion.
Yesterday it was Anita.
Today it is Elena.
Who will it be tomorrow?

ON THE WAY TO COLLEGE

At the end of the corridor, I saw her stepping off the escalator and entering Westmount Square. It was she! I had not wanted to meet anyone, especially her; but a longing possessed me now. To get to the top faster, I avoided the escalator and walked up the stairs. Going through the door, she too noticed me and waited.

"Hi!" she said and was cold in her way.

"Hi!" I grumbled. I was afraid to speak. Would my mouth show?

"How are you?"

"Fine. And you?

"My eyes hurt. It must have been in the metro." She had a white paper tissue in her hand and was rubbing an eye. The corners of her eye were red.

"Fog?" I still did not dare to speak much and led the way, as we turned right.

"Yeah! Probably.... What's new with you?"

"I thought I had seen you in the train." When I had gotten on at the McGill station.

"Yeah, I was in the... metro."

"It was your coat I saw."

"Ah, my coat! It's very..., eh?" She touched her coat at the shoulder as to mean its color.

"Not so much because of that." I had become confident with my possibility to speak now". "Oh, you know why. It's because it's your..."

"Oh, my coat, yes! Because it's mine, eh?"

"Yeah. Your coat! Because it's yours."

"How many classes do you have today?" she said.

"Only one." They went to the right, through the first Westmount Square west exit doors. "I had an English class this morning, but I missed it."

"Yeah?"

"I had to go 'n' see the dentist. I'm coming from there now. I thought you had noticed. Because of my mouth! Doesn't it show?" I raised my face towards her, my mouth loose, to let her see. We were on the escalator. She was standing a step higher, to my left.

"I hadn't noticed."

I tried to pull one of the left doors. They were locked.

"The other door," she said.

Other people who had walked up were exiting with us. I stopped to let a lady pass after her.

"Where are you?" she said and turned. "Ah, you're there! You're not fast."

I pulled the hood of my army coat over my head. She had already done the same with her coat. I hurried behind her to walk at her right. My frozen right cheek would be safer from her glances there. "Are you in a hurry?" I asked. "Do you have a class?"

"No. It's just... this is the way I am. I'm always walking fast when I'm alone."

We walked in silence for a tract of sidewalk. Then I said, "So! How's your morale, nowadays?"

"Morale?"

"Morale. It's spelled M-O-R-A-L-E. The stress is on the second syllable."

We were crossing St. Catherine Street. "Oh! Morale!" she exclaimed.

"Yes. Morale." We were waiting in the street for a car to pass ahead. "How is your morale nowadays?"

Drawing in air through her mouth, she produced a clicking sound that was so peculiar of her. "Ah, you!"

"What do you mean by that 'naughty-naughty'?"

My bag touched her. I shifted it to my right hand. "What is it you want to tell me?" she said. "If you have something on your mind, say it!"

My mind was assailed by a sense of pleasure. "Perhaps. There's something I'd like very much to say to you."

"You would like to? Say it, then!"

"But I don't know how you would take it, how your response would be."

"Oh! Say it! Don't worry. You won't hurt me. I have a strong heart." She pointed to her heart under the purplish red coat.

"Okay! Here it is, then. Would you like to go out with me this weekend?"

We prepared to cross Dorchester Blvd. "Didn't you want to tell me something about my morale?"

"I thought this was what you wanted... I misunderstood you."

We reached the other side of the Boulevard. "Now! Why did you jump from morale to this?"

"I thought this was what you wanted me to say. I misunderstood you. Anyway, it doesn't matter. What's your answer?"

"You didn't answer my question and I won't answer yours."

"But..." I wanted to insist and then I abstained. I had to let her talk. "What is it you want to know?"

She attacked the question with novel eagerness. "Why did you change the argument? Didn't you want to say, didn't you want to hear from me why I was prejudiced against Italians?"

I turned my head to look at her in the face. "Why you were...?"

"Why I was prejudiced against Italians."

"I never thought that of you."

"Didn't you mean that with your question? I thought, I believed, from the way you behaved, that you..."

"Come on! Who did you take me for? Why would I think a thing like that?"

"Yes, I know. But..."

"Why should I think that you're prejudiced against Italians? To me, we're all part of the same earth." I was searching in my mind to better express my feelings about the subject. "What do I care if you're Greek, Italian, or French?"

"Yeah. But you must have thought that my origins are Greek?"

We had come under the railway bridge and were starting to cross Greene Avenue. "Oh yeah, that yes! But only in the sense that you were brought up in a different culture! And, for that, I welcome you even more. The rest doesn't matter."

"What did you mean, then, when you...?"

"When I asked you about your morale, I meant your self-confidence, not your morality. It was a misunderstanding." The hood of her coat had slipped from her head. Seeing her naked, smooth, long hair generated in me a greater feeling of her frailty. I had the urge to set her hood back over her head and say, 'There! Your hood slipped back!' But then I thought that perhaps she wanted it that way. The air was not very cold, and the flurry of before had since stopped. "What I want to know from you is, and I'll ask it again: Would you like to go out with me this weekend?" I noticed a much sweeter tone in my voice this time, as I was saying the same words all over again.

We were walking under the new Trans-Canada Highway. "No. I can't. I'm sorry. I already go out with a guy."

"When? How?" I stammered.

"Look!" She became playful. "Didn't you see the ring on my finger?" She raised her left hand to have it well in view and let me see.

"When?"

"When was this?"

"Yeah. When did this happen?"

"I was going out with him this summer. We broke off, and then, at Christmas, this Christmas, when we met, we made peace and we started going out together again."

"Where is he?"

"Where is he now, you mean?"

"Well, yeah. No, I mean, does he come here, to Dawson, or is he...?"

"He goes to McGill. You should see! He's terrific. Not like me..."

A lady, faraway and coming towards us on the sidewalk, shouted something. I didn't hear. She gestured to me to look behind us. I turned and saw a small bulldozer on the sidewalk and coming at full speed behind us. We quickly took repair between two parked cars. I raised my arm and nodded to the lady who had warned us. We paid attention to the incoming traffic and crossed Selby Street. And when we got on the opposite sidewalk, I said, "And I suppose you wouldn't give me a chance, or would you? The fact that you have a boyfriend doesn't mean you can't go out with me?"

"No, I can't. I mean you have to break off the engagement." I had stopped. "Which way are you going?"

"This way." I pointed to the wooden stairway leading from Selby Street to the main entrance of the college building.

"Okay. But if I slip and I'm about to break my neck, you'll have to hold me, then!"

"Oh, sure! That and more... for you." But I noticed there was no danger. The usual path on the wide staircase had been cleared of the snow.

"You know I can't," she continued. "You would do the same if it were you."

"All I know is that you're unfair to me."

"Unfair to you? You know the way it is. It must be the same in Italy too. Tell me the way they go about it in Italy."

"We'd better not talk about it."

"Ah, you see? It is the same. You are very free in your thinking, but you have to consider that others..."

"What do you want me to say? If you're happy, I'm happy too." We had come to the bottom of the stairway. As I spoke I considered the distance that separated us from the entrance. I had to say something good before we entered the building. And I was aware not to step on the soft muddy snow where it had piled up. "The fact is that I like you very much and I thought that, perhaps, who knows, something of good might have come between us? You are the only girl in the whole college who touched me." I shook one of the left doors but it would not open. I quickly shifted to the right doors to open one for her.

Going through the open door, she said, "When I first understood that you were... I tried to make you understand."

"Yes, you tried and made me believe who knows what. You never did it in a direct way."

We had passed through the second set of doors, always to the right, and turning left to walk up the staircase. "I couldn't tell you! It's not me! I don't like to tell a guy..."

"Yeah! I know. All women are like this. Like all other women, you are... Women are ambiguous."

"Yes."

We were on the second floor and turned left. There were few students in the lounge to our left. There was no one in the hallway. "I guess, a woman doesn't like to tell a guy who's courting her she doesn't like him in a direct way."

We stood by the lockers. She said, "Is your morale better now?"

"Yes... because I talked to you. But, don't worry about me. What's important in all this is that you're happy. You're happy?" She took time to nod. "Nothing else matters, then."

I went to my locker and I was about to open it when she said, "What's the combination of your locker? I forgot it. You know, I have three lockers where I can put my coat!"

"The combination is seven, twelve, thirty-one, if I'm right. Come, I'll show you. Perhaps it's easier to remember on the lock." I started dialing. "Seven... twelve... thirty-one. You know, for the last number, even if you don't get exactly thirty-one, it opens just the same," the lock did not open at thirty, "sometimes."

"Ha! ha! Sometimes?"

The locker was open. "You know you can use this locker, there's lots of room now, because the guy I shared it with, I don't see him anymore, it seems he's quit school."

"Yes," she said, and as in a reflection I heard her continue, "I won't let you sketch me again. Because when you draw me, you take away my soul, you take part of my soul away from me."

"Oh no, you're wrong there! That's my soul, not yours."

"No, it's my soul. It's my picture you're drawing!"

"Yes, your picture, but it's my feelings that go into its making. It's me who draws you. You're just the inspiration, that's all."

"No. I..."

"Come on, it's not like a photograph." I gestured with my hands as if taking a snapshot.

"Yes, I know, but still it's my soul that..."

"It's all right. If you don't want me to draw you, I won't."

I turned to the locker to hang my coat and put on my jacket I had in it. She seemed to be disappointed but then, as if coming from a reverie, she said, "The only times I had my picture taken was when I finished school."

"Finished school?"

"When I finished High School, when I graduated; and this summer, when I became a Canadian citizen."

He wanted to say that he too wanted to take the Canadian citizenship now that he could. But she suddenly remembered something, started going towards the end of the hallway, and said, "Wait for me! I want to see if…"

"Do you have a class now?" I said.

"No, I don't. Do you?"

"No!"

"I'm just going… I want to see if someone is there, Wait…"

At the end of the hallway I saw her look into a classroom through the door window. When she came back, I said, "Come on, put your coat in the locker. Don't you think…, because of what I told you. We can still be friends, great friends. Take your coat off. I'll hold your books for you."

Her coat, hung by the hood, just about touched the bottom of the locker. She then took her books back from me. "What did you say the combination was? I'd better write it down so I won't forget it. It's seven…"

She had written seventeen on her notebook cover. "It's seven, not seventeen."

"Yes, I know. But… so they'll think it's a phone number." She crossed out the 1.

"Oh, a guy's locker, I see." I gave her the rest of the combination. She added one more casual digit to make it into a phone number. Then, she was about to lock the locker, when I said, "Wait! Wait! Don't lock it!" I wanted to get my German book but, then, I thought I would go to the washroom first. "It's all right, you can lock it. I'll get my book later"

She tried but couldn't make the lock work. "You better do it. You're stronger."

"Aha!" And she helped me by pushing the door. After a while I thought about something and said, "Oh, by the way, are you taking all your ten courses here, at Dawson?"

"No, only eight. I was taking two more courses at McGill but I dropped those."

"Why?"

"It was too much work."

"Yeah... I take seven and I am in a mess."

A group of students was passing by, arguing, and disrupting the quiet from before. "Oh, no, my teacher!" she said. "He's coming this way. I don't want him to see me. Wait!" She went among the students to get to the other side and take cover by the fountain of the lounge. I tried to figure out which one was her teacher. When the group had dispersed, she came back to me. "It wasn't him.... Wait! I want to see if he's there."

She went to the end of the hallway again. I waited, looked at the fountain and at her. I felt my mouth sticky. A few more students passed by. She was still there. I went to drink. I had already drunk when she joined me by the fountain. "Do you have a course at twelve?" I asked.

"Yes. You too."

"Yes."

"Are you coming to the library?"

"Yes, but first I have to go to the washroom."

"Nature calls, eh?"

"Yeah." But I was thinking of combing my hair.

"I'm going to the library, Achille."

"Okay! I'll find you there, **Elena, my friend**." And I touched her shoulder, lightly. That one time I drew her picture, when I touched her chin to have her face in the right view, she had recoiled from me.

As she was going towards the library, I turned the corner to go into the washroom. In front of the mirror, I noticed my disheveled hair. This girl had treated me so sweetly in spite of that! My mouth was not in as bad a shape as I had thought. I looked at my new filling. My cheek was still frozen. It did not hurt now. It was going to hurt later, when I'd think about it. I knew that. And by that I didn't mean my tooth.

7D. My Friend Vicky

HOW DO I GAIN YOUR LOVE?

I was telling Vicky
of my confusion re her.
Once again, tonight,
I find I am wrong.

Why am I torturing you?
This is not the way
to friendship or love.
What a regret! Again.

And, what is worse,
I find I haven't found
what I deluded myself
I had already located.

Vicky! What is the price to pay?
What is the pain I must endure?
What wisdom must I come to
in order to find and gain your love?

SECONDARY CHARACTERS

Johnny	Achille's rival
Silvia	Johnny's girlfriend
Rose	Vicky's friend
Eva	Vicky's friend
Caroline	Achille's friend
Nikos	Achille's friend
Patrick	Achille's friend
Herr H	German instructor
Sabine	German tutor
Annie	classmate

In College, I befriended and romantically pursued **Vicky**. She was fickle with the way she related to me. When I wanted to be more than friends, she wanted to be just friends. Contrariwise, when I behaved like a friend, she wanted me to be more than a friend.

WITH FRIENDS LIKE THESE ...
Then, I went to eat. In the cafeteria, I saw Vicky, my friend, with her friends. I passed behind her when I went to get my orange drink. Coming back I touched her shoulder with the two straws in my hand.

As she turned, I said, "Are you coming to see Sabine?" Sabine was the German tutor.

She recognized me. Her face brightened and greeted me with a lively "Oh! Hi!"

I didn't answer to her "Hi!". I persisted with my question, "Are you coming to see Sabine?"

Her face became serious. Was she regretting the enthusiasm she'd shown in seeing me? "I don't think so!" she said, with her breath coming to a pause so typical of her. "Nooo!" she continued and lingered on her answer to give herself time to think and then rally and attack the next thought, "I... Are you going?"

"If I have time, I'll go." Always with the same unpleasant attitude, I was already leaving, dispersing the words behind me with each step forward and away from her, not saying goodbye or the like.

I wasn't going to sit at her table. This I had decided before. There was no time to waste if was going to see Sabine and all that that was to follow. Besides, her table was packed! Imagine me sitting and eating my hamburger at the edge of their table, when I wanted all the comfort imaginable, a whole table to myself. The main thing was to sit in satisfaction of space, but mostly, what I wanted, and this is the main reason, I wanted to sit at ease, at ease with myself, not to be constrained with the presence of others, as I was eating with time pressing, weighing on me at the tick-tock of each minute. And the best way to do this was to be a snob to everybody or treat things with detachment. Those people have nothing to do with me and my life, my emotions, the attention I need, my longing to love … I needed to see the way and not the people. It is like wearing **hackney's blinds**. It is a horrible, gloomy vision of the world, as if I were really wearing blinds, as if I were deprived of peripheral vision, seeing clearly only the path in front of me. *But if I don't do it, what happens? It strips me; it strips me of my will, of what I want to do.*

Of all this I was thinking, or more properly, just feeling, as I was sitting all by myself not too far from her, their table. I didn't check our respective positions to see if she was facing me. I would not glance towards her direction, as I was very effectively making grandiose use of my hackney's blinds. Even though, I was convinced that my reasoning, my logics, and my motives were right, here I was torturing myself, thinking about my rude and unjust behavior to her: her face becoming radiant on seeing me, her fantastic "Hi!" to me, my not saying hi to her, my going away without saying bye, and my asking her, "Are you coming to see Sabine!" should have been 'going', not 'coming'!

Leaving her without saying bye was unjust, even if I could justify my not sitting at their table. The table was already fully packed all around it! And it could have been more justifiable if I would have been sitting with someone else. If there had been someone else waiting for me to sit together with! But there I was, all alone. I've been sitting with them other times and played cards with them. But her friends are foreign to me and I am a foreigner to them!

Her friends are Silvia, Rose, Eva, and Johnny. If they do something for me, that one thing, letting me enter in their cards' game, they do it only because of her, because of my being with her. Certainly, I'm not going to blame them. It is their group, their privacy, where they belong. They defend and guard their in-group from outsiders, and that is well! I can understand that! But where does that leave me?

Something else enhanced my internal torture. Just when I had understood her role, in the library at the Richelieu campus, she refused my offering to wait for her. "Don't be silly!" she said. *Don't force yourself into other people's lives.* My wailing is pathetic. Even so, it goes unanswered. Was it because of my hurt ego that I held a grudge against her? In the library she told me, "You're not going to be mad at me, are you?" "Okay! Okay!" I answered, with a dry tone in my voice. The more I thought about her, the more I found myself drawn to her. Now, the one who was going to pay was I. It was all because of my unrequited love for her. *Oh, please, Vicky! What are you afraid of? That I might corrupt you? Let me love you! Glucklich allein ist die Seele, die liebt!* (But happy is the soul that lives!)

On the way to the Richelieu campus with all the white and mushy snow around and under our boots, I'll ask her, "Tell me what you meant by that 'Don't be silly!' Be sincere and tell me the truth."

Unexpectedly, Michel appeared in front of me. I remembered that if someone was going to sit with me, I could explain my not sitting at their table. When I received him, I was unemotional outwardly but enthusiastic inwardly. And there was one more reason to be happy. In being busy with him, however trivial and uninteresting, I wasn't going to think about her as I had been doing.

So, with Michel, I was cheered up, even if somewhat artificially. Then, unfortunately, I had to leave him. He was still eating his salad sandwich. Crossing the cafeteria, even now I didn't look or felt the need to look in the direction of her table. As a matter of fact, I made it sure that I would not. And I was conscious of my countenance and demeanor, with my left hand in the pocket in my army coat, as I went through the chairs and tables of the cafeteria. 'Caf' she called it when referring to the Richelieu one.

On my way to Richelieu to see Sabine, I'd reached the bus stop at the corner of Couvent Street, when I thought of what I would tell her when we would next meet in the German class, to explain my behavior in the cafeteria. "Are you never in a mood," I would say, "when you wish to be alone, all by yourself?" (My friend Fanny told me that once.) "I was in a bad mood and I was in a hurry for all the things I had to do."

Thinking that this would not be enough, I also imagined of telling her, "I feel as though I've been cheated. You in the library, me looking for and in quest of a friend, and you speaking to me that way, "Don't be silly!" Why must it be that you cannot love me? My fear is contained in this feeling of my being a fool, playing the fool after you, rendering myself ridiculous for my love for you. It is the cause of this feeling that makes you want to blot out everything, not to care anymore, put an end to this search for friendship, love. To blot out everything and, what remains, is the passion of my life. But I vegetate. I wallow in the apathy and indifference of life. In other words, I am lost, yes, I'm lost because my soul has stopped striving to be unique, my soul has given up, alas, to that reality and vision of life that still might be, that which my soul has hoped for, for so many years! My soul has done all this 'to be free', not to be enslaved, not to become a sheep, to preserve within itself that wolfish character that makes it me."

Imagining of telling her this when we meet again in the German class, or, later, in the library, when on meeting me she would be sulky at me, and I would do all this to win her back. To win her back!

... WHO NEEDS ENEMIES?

Monday, February 14, 1972. Vicky wore a daring mini skirt today. Splendid legs! I saw the marks left on her legs by the chair when, at the end of the German class, she was going up the stairs to her Math class. "Bye, then!" I said. *Smile! Give me a smile, sweet girl!*

Tuesday, February 15. I found her by her locker with Silvia and Rose this morning. Later, I went for my Canadian citizenship. It didn't take me long and I went back for my German class. And, at the end of class, I went to the caf to eat her orange and then on the way home talked about her aspirations and masturbation. She was so sweet to me. *O Vicky!*

Wednesday, February 16. It started as a fine day, like the fine day it was weather-wise. I wanted to go and see Fanny, my friend. I was a little late and I went to see Sabine, the German tutor, and I missed my Eastern Religions class and Fanny.

Vicky, with her orange, went out of the German classroom at the five-minute break. I joined her. She told me she had to wait for Rose. I wanted to pass through Westmount Square to see about the book Mrs. P had told me about.

After class, I said I wouldn't stay. Rose was waiting by the locker. "You said you wouldn't stay. Why are coming with me?" she said. "Okay! Goodbye!" "No! No! No!" *Those beautiful eyes!*

We walked to the Selby campus. In the caf she paid me a drink. We played Hearts. We were wasting time. I should've never stayed.

Walking to the subway, I was afraid of stepping on my own feet. I walked like a mannequin. I was not at ease. In the bookstore, we did not find the book. I didn't remember the name of the author. We met shy Josie in the corridor.

I realized that Vicky's behavior with me is different when we're all alone. When we're with other people, it looks like I don't exist. The same thing happened last night at the Goethe House. If I talk to someone else, if my eyes aren't only for her, I become a stranger to her.

Thursday, February 17. I met Vicky at the Berri-de-Montigny metro station. On the 90 bus, I told her about her indifference towards me whenever we are in the company of others. 'Love is a fight for dominance,' I was thinking in the cafeteria, after offering her and her friends a drink. *Give in, Vicky, to my dominance of you!* I noticed she had been sweet, sweeter than ever with me! Fake? In the library afterwards, she told she had the Math and the Italian test to send in with her university application.

Monday, February 21. After the German test on word order, we went to the cafeteria. She wanted to eat her orange, which she shared with me. She was ever so sweet. How is it possible for one not to love her? I had given her the book *The Sensuous Woman*. We talked about what makes a best seller, about her being frustrated for having to read *Midsummer's Night Dream*, and about Goethe's seeing love as a carrier of life in his poem *Freudvoll und Leidvoll*, etc. Oh, Vicky!

Tuesday, February 22. I was sitting in the cafeteria with Mauro. When he went to get his piece of pie, Vicky stopped by. She had her break from her three-hour-long Humanities class. Ever sweet! But what did she do with my scarf in the Richelieu locker?

Rose was sulky with me when I asked her about Vicky in the library before. One more of her standoffish moods! Insignificant guy like me! But Silvia and Eva, sitting nearby, were nice.

I met Annie in Sabine's office. She told me of her zest for life. "My heart fills with joy," she said.

Wednesday, February 23. I wanted Vicky to wait for me because I wanted to ask Herr H about Vladimir's final exam. "I have to go. Sorry!" she said. I approached the teacher's desk. Then, as I was coming out of the classroom, she said bye and went to the bathroom.

Friday, February 25. At the locker, as I was taking my winter shirt off, I saw Rose coming. She said that Vicky had just left. She was somewhat polite, maybe because she was using our locker.

I met Vicky in the Selby cafeteria. She had not gone home after all. She carried a tray of food. She asked me if I was going to eat. I said, "No!" We said bye. I was mad at her because she shunned me on Wednesday. What I wanted to do was to conquer my feelings for her. *There's nothing I'm going to get from her.* Yet, my heart bleeds for just thinking about her.

Still in the cafeteria, I went to change my quarter to do photocopies of my High School Leaving Certificate, I heard my name called out, "Achille!" It was JoAnne, the blond girl. She was sitting at a table with a lot of boyish stallions. She wore black with her stout thighs, red lipstick, and blond hair. She was radiant and I told her, but she didn't hear. She was off from McGill, just for today. She sensed, I guess, my lack of interest for her. "Okay!" I said, as to say, "Stop!" and said goodbye.

Monday, February 28. After my Humanities class at the Dome, and after I got very cold outside, I met Vicky and friends at the Richelieu building main exit door. The German class had been cancelled. I went to the Selby campus. I wanted to eat, as I told her; but, instead, I went home with her and Silvia and Rose. She came through Westmount Square with me while her friends went from outside. We met them after in Alexis Nihon Plaza because of some shopping that Vicky and Rose had to do. She gave me back *The Sensuous Woman* book. I gave her to read a short story I had been writing. I had taken it out of my journal while going through the Westmount Square corridor. She'd chosen me instead of her friends! *Why do you give me so much, Vicky, and when I come to you, you push me away?*

Tuesday, March 7. Vicky was absent for the German class. Annie was sweet when I asked her about the homework. I hadn't done it.

Wednesday, March 15. The sword is again in my hand. I feel its handle in my palm. It wants to come down and slice things up. It was on the Sauvé bus, while I was coming back from school, that I had this image of the sword. Why? Was if because of Vicky?

After a lousy German test, I was walking towards the Selby campus with Vicky. We started arguing about the meaning of the story *An der Brücke* by Böll. Then, she would not let me explain certain things I wanted to say regarding her. They had to do with …

(1) When, in the metro with Silvia and Eva, I stated that marriages undergo fewer complications if they are between people of the same language and customs. I wanted to mention that Nietzsche said, "People of the same mother tongue and nation can share of a greater number of experiences."

(2) When, on Monday, she was to get off at Jean Talon and I had no time to explain to her my jealousy when she said she'd remain for a whole hour all alone with Mr. G. I wanted to explain that I was jealous because I cared for her.

And (3) all the times she hurt me when she used to tell me of her boyfriend and the appointments she had with him right after the German class. "I'm sorry," she would say, for not coming with me. I wanted to say that I was there for her all the time. When she wanted me to keep her company, I was there; but, she didn't care when I was left alone, like a dog!

She said that I was a nitpicker. And what else did she call me in the metro? I can't recall presently. I said I wanted to see a picture of her boyfriend.

At Selby, my friend Fanny was by her locker. "*Bongiorno!*" she said to me. Vicky went to her locker to meet Silvia. I stopped and talked with Fanny. She was very open and friendly, when I thought that she was angry with me. I was in a bad mood, but not for long. Fanny makes me feel good. She's always there for me. *O Fanny, my friend, no one has ever understood me as well as you!*

I left Fanny. She was going to meet a girlfriend. And I went by Vicky's locker. Silvia was there. She wanted to go and look in the library, but just then Vicky was coming. I said I had been looking for her. She got her books and said bye. She had a class.

On the way to the subway, she was bringing me in their conversation and saying my name almost every time she talked to me. She was trying to be nice to me because I had told her that she was not nice to me when we were with company. Was this hypocrisy that made me hate her later?

At home, my cousins were over. Tony told stories about his courting Lina, his wife. Lina was sweet. She trusts I will succeed in school? "Do you really think so, Li?" Oh, the dark side of me! Will I ever be to their expectations? It is a dream, an ideal, and not all ideals have known their light.

Tuesday, March 21. This morning, I was late for my philosophy class, I met my future lover Debbie in the cafeteria, and I went to the library later. Vicky came by for her break from the meditation class. She's more attentive to me now.

After Vicky left, my trying to convince beautiful Nada to pose for me failed and this set my mood for the rest of the day. I showed a lack of confidence with Sabine, my German tutor.

On the way to the Richelieu campus, I met my friend Fanny. She was nice.

Monday, April 3. This morning I gave a presentation on the Will to Power in the philosophy class to prove that suicide in not a choice, but a non-choice. It was a very angry, domineering presentation, a will to power. I told Bob, "You shut up or get out!" And I was arguing with Carl. He would not leave me alone because I too had not been receptive to his presentation. The will to power in his vengeance was greater that his will to power in his trying to understand. I guess, with my high-handed behavior, I ruined my image, the way she thought of me, in the eyes of my future lover Bree. Did I prove my point? The interest of the two guys was power to me.

Charged with my will to power I went to the library. Silvia, who was getting more friendly and sweeter every day that went by, Rose, and Eva were there. Later, Vicky came. She told me of the way Herr H had asked her about me, "Where's your friend?" "How do I know?" was her answer. She gave me to understand the old man had put "ideas" in his head. I had been absent because there had been one other meeting in the Selby cafeteria about the teachers declassification. I asked about the homework that had been assigned.

Johnny, Silvia's boyfriend, appeared on the other side of the glass division. Both of them, Vicky and Johnny, communicated in mime through the glass division. It was about her having given him her picture. He called Vicky to him. She went to him. "Don't tell anybody. Today's my birthday," he'd told her. Vicky went with him. Sulkiness, unhappiness, and jealousy were taking possession of me; but, then, I was revived, I was charged with the will to power, with the help of Silvia and Rose, who made a joke about Johnny.

What game is Vicky playing, by the way? Is she competing with Silvia? Or, does she want me jealous because she's jealous when I engage with another girl? With all probability, that was it, because of what happened later with Caroline.

When she was away with Johnny; Caroline, Nikos girlfriend, appeared on the other side of the glass division. She was joyous, content to see me. She came over and sat where Vicky had been sitting. With her, it is different. She's no jack-of-all-trades like Vicky. She gave all her attention to me and me alone.

When Vicky and Johnny came back, Vicky had to take another chair at another table to sit down. She didn't like it, I could tell. I could see hostility against me already showing. "Sit on her lap!" was Eva's comment. She meant Caroline's lap. The conversation between Caroline and me was sort of private. When I made the introduction to the Italian gang, I found out that Eva was Greek. Rose had left. I was observing Johnny's approach towards Silvia. "She likes it," I said and thought of the power of courting. "I didn't say I didn't like it," was Silvia's answer. Then, when he approached Eva, I heard Silvia saying, "And Caroline?" I noticed that Caroline felt uneasy. I proposed to her to go for a hot chocolate down to the cafeteria. She would take a tea instead. And off we went. "So long!" Vicky answered with a sour "Bye!" I was conscious of what I was doing. I knew I wanted Caroline's whole attention for me. What was there to save, anyway?

In the cafeteria we talked about relationships and making the other the target of one's will to power. "I don't want power," she said. Was it a negation of her will to power or idealism?

And who showed up? Patrick! I introduced him. Caroline left. She had to see a friend who was getting married. Patrick told me about his problems, his missed VD. We were going to the library, passing not too far from their table in the cafeteria. Silvia and Eva waved. I didn't see Vicky and I didn't look for her.

In the library, Nikos, Caroline's boyfriend, was there. We were talking about Buber's *I-thou relation* and Kierkegaard's *infinitely interested in the reality of another* and saying that it was the same thing. I noticed we were boring Patrick. I made a mental note to read the *I-thou* book in the summer.

Left Nikos and went to the Italian club upstairs on the forth floor. On the way up Patrick met a friend of his. In the Italian club, the lights were out. They were dancing in the dark. While standing in there in all uneasiness, I was trying to recognize the faces of the women in there. I imagined Vicky as one the girls dancing in there. What we had there was the shy and the sly. In my innocence and naiveté I could never fathom what the sly would do. Very sick! I had lost my power, my cool. Luckily Patrick came and said he wanted to go. What a joint! *My God! What is this? What nest of wasps did I fall into?*

Vicky was out there with Johnny and Eva. Johnny said, "Achille, you were in there?" I didn't answer him. I said to Vicky, "You come here? Aren't you ashamed?" She didn't answer me.

We left. They were walking in front of us. "I want to see the third floor," Eva said. I said to Patrick that I would be going home now. I said, "Bye, everyone!" She didn't say bye! She didn't even pay attention to me. The others did but it wasn't like the other times. I was going to my locker. Johnny had his arm around Eva's shoulders.

Fucking friend! She was angry now because I deprived her of my power on the day of her friend's visit to the college, in front of her friends. Did she want me to tend to her and follow her wherever she went? But what did I want from you, uh? "Let's be friends!" you said. *So you can look for or go with others!* And now you sulk?

Monday, April 10. I had a **fight** with Johnny in the Selby cafeteria today. It was just wrestling really. I had to do it. After all this time without fighting, some 'inflated' kid who thought himself big pushed me into it. I didn't want to fight. What I regretted most was that I was fighting in school, which to me was unacceptable.

It started with him flinging cards at Rose. I wanted to go home and I picked the cards myself because Rose wouldn't do it. He said, "Achille, you shouldn't have done it." I said, "Oh, shut up!" but always in the sense and the way it is used with friends. However, because he did not see me as a friend, this incensed 'what's-his-name'. He got up, went around the table, and came face to face with me. *Poor little Achille, all we need to say is "woof!" and he runs off and cowers. What made you think that you could control me, 'friend'?* "What did you say, boy?" he said. He insisted with the same question. I would not retreat to his advancing. He pushed me. I pushed him back. He would not desist. I threw him on the floor twice. The second time was better. I had his head locked in my arm, the little thing. What was he trying to prove? Then, I let go of him and we were up. He pushed me against the chairs and tables and put up his fists. That's what they do in the movies, but real life is no movie. Then, this girl, from the other side of the cafeteria, called him off. She came up and ordered us to stop fighting. A woman of character! I bow to you girl. Our will to not fight prevailed. We stopped fighting.

It was entirely your fault, Vicky. You who, with your stupid childish behavior, tried to make me jealous! It was you who brought forth all this. All this was not necessary. It could've been prevented. You're happy, now? I might be partly mistaken but not completely wrong. And, then, going away from the scene, from what was happening, from us, with Silvia and Rose, to save face. The woman who stopped us, that's the girl I respect. Why didn't you do the same? I was more to you than to that girl. You've seen and heard the last of me, Vicky. Cheap people! Why did I have to be mixed up with them?

Today I wanted to tell you that you are my muse, my drive, in my writing. But with you retreating from me during the fight, I retreat from you now. This was what had to happen to destroy completely my feelings for you, especially by your angry attitude towards me in the German class and later on our way to Selby leaving me out, yet again! Annie was much more attentive towards me than you when she said, "Why don't you say anything, Achille?"

Friday, April 13. Today I was supposed to do my presentation on Leopardi in the Poetry class. But there were no classes. Teachers went to Quebec City to protest about teachers' reclassification.

The first time I was at Richelieu for my Religion class, I talked to the Trinidadian girl in the study room. I went to Selby with her. I sat all alone in the cafeteria and wrote about the Will to Power. My nemesis, Johnny, passed by several times; as usual looking for female companionship here and there and everyone gets that 'friendly' arm of his around her shoulders. When I stood to go to the library, Eva was there. She was looking for Johnny and (*Isn't that ironic?*) she asked me to find him for her. I said he was there before. As we came out of the cafeteria, he was there in the hallway. It seemed she wanted to continue and come with me, but then she went to him. *Is she near-sighted?*

Nobody I knew was in the library. I went to the Richelieu campus again to make sure there would be no Poetry class. No, there would be no class presentation for me, today! I ate my lunch in the cafeteria there. Then I went up to the forth floor. What if Vicky was there? She wasn't in the Statistics lab. As I was passing in front of the study room, just two or three people were in there. And I noticed this one girl reading all by herself. I opened the door. It was Vicky! I approached her. I wanted to have an explanation from her. I sat on the table and I said, "I am angry at you, you know!"

"You're always angry that it doesn't shock anymore," she said.

"I am always angry?" and it started from there. Regarding the fight with Johnny, she was 'shocked' that I considered it to be her fault.

She showed me the ring she'd put in her necklace. Johnny had given it to her. This was done after the fight. "You don't know Johnny. He's a human being. You don't know him."

Cheap people! Not so much for me, because she says that she told me, but for what she did to her 'friend' Silvia, Johnny's girlfriend.

And don't say that you never led me on? On the day of the Italian class she made me sit next to her in the classroom and she made me stand by her in the subway train.

Fucken 'friend'! Cheap!

And what happened to the boyfriend she supposedly had?

She said she resented that I tried to change her. She mentioned the book *The Sensuous Woman* I gave her to read and the time I wanted to bring her to Brian's place.

Is she dumb? About the book she's right, if new knowledge means change; but my wanting to bring her to my friend's place was because I wanted to show her off, not because I wanted to change her. Dumb!

You don't know, Vicky, that a big joke is being played on you. You should know about the will to power to understand. I can explain it to you. You want to overpower Johnny on account of the superficial Don Juan that he is. But you cannot possess him because he is like that. He's in search for the many not for the one. I might be wrong, but if I am not, you're the one who is going to be hurt. The question is, "Is he a libertine or only a showman?" He can't ever be yours, Vicky, if he is a libertine.

Rot as much as you like, now! You're alone, for the way you've treated Silvia and me. You're no longer my friend!

I so regret having opened up myself to you, telling you about my feelings, for treating you like a friend!

What must be decided now is how I'm going to treat you these remaining days left before the end of the school year. Am I going to treat you as a stranger, pretending that you don't count? Or, am I going to treat you as a friend, pretending that nothing happened? I like to give myself a different possibility, but I already know how it's going to go, because, I am not very forgiving. I believe in the will to power, and I am going to follow my feelings. No phony face with me. I was down and you kicked me! Do you think it is right to take Johnny as your boyfriend, after I've had a fight with him? Or, was it to put me down because I was no longer in love with you? But you won't admit any of this. That would go against your appearance, your façade, your image. You were not a friend. I deluded myself in thinking that you could be.

(This had to happen with Vicky. Without this downfall, I would've never got to know my future lover Bree, the epitome of the fair sex in my life.)

Wednesday, April 19. I got on the bus with the German 401 gang and the girl from the Religion class. And it was with her that I conversed till our stop at Mountain-Drummond. When Heather said hi, Vicky turned towards me. I was standing right behind her. She gave me a marvelous hi, sunny as the day. I just nodded. You can't afford it, eh? I meant my sullen face. And it was like that for the rest of our outing to see Böll's show with Herr H. I avoided any contact with her, and she did the same, I suppose.

After the show, I passed by her and her friends Rose and Eva, as I was going to the subway station, on de Maisonneuve. I had walked down with Heather. They pretended not to notice us.

8A. My Lover Debbie

MY KIND OF WOMAN
It'd begun at the bus stop
she stood self-assured
and wore a trench coat
with a fishing net cap,
like in the Mata-Hari movie
I'd watched the night before.
From the short 'snout',
I knew it was her,
the kind that I liked!

ON THE MOUNTAIN
I went to college at the time. I was waiting in the metro station with uneasiness. I thought of going to the other side when I saw her.

"Hi!" she said.

"Hi!" I said. "Did you see me?"

"Yes, I saw you. I was on the other side."

I didn't do what I'd proposed to do: Smack her on the lips and say, "Thank you for being here." And I'd imagined her saying, "What was that for?" And I would've said, "For keeping the appointment, for caring, for being here."

"You said you were going shopping," I said. "What did you buy?"

"I didn't. I went to my aunt's."

"Did you eat?"

"Yes."

"Because the first thing I wanted to say to you was if you wanted to go and eat something."

"No. I've had my supper."

Instinctively we were walking to get out of the station.

"Where are we going?" she asked.

"I don't know. Where would you like to go? If you have anything special you'd want me to bring you to…"

"No. I don't know. You decide."

"I thought... What do you say if we go to Mont Royal?"

"Okay. It's all right with me."

She flushed at the suggested place and what it implied. It implied necking and petting. And I was uneasy too.

"Good! Let's go, then!" I said.

We turned around and went down the stairs, returning on the platform, to wait for the train. We changed line at Berri-de-Montigny. When we got on the next train, we were standing. I offered her to stand with me, but she said, "Why?"

"To stay together," I said. But she remained standing where she was.

Then, just later on, someone got off and she was able to sit down and I stood next to her.

I noticed her necklace and said, "That's the star of Israel, right?"

"Yes," she said.

When we got off at our station, we had to walk a long platform to get to the exit at the far end of it. She kept swinging her arm. Without saying anything, I held her hand. Her fingers coiled around mine. And we played with our fingers.

With a more agreeable sensation and with a less disagreeable uneasiness, we got out of the metro station. And soon after we got on the bus that was to take us near the mountain's eastern slope.

As we moved to the back of the bus to sit right on the very last seat, I remembered Luisita. "Boy, are you tall!" she'd said, as I was about to join her. I got the same feeling that she would say the same thing to me. I hoped of finding one of those seats, and I did. It sank under me. Just what I needed! I was at eye level with her now. The difference was not uncomfortable. Was she taller than Luisita?

When we got off the bus, we walked uphill towards the top of the mountain. I had my arm around her. We came to the outskirts of a playground. It was deserted.

We crossed the playground. She took off her glasses and put them in her purse. Under a tree, somewhat secluded, I kissed her. Those voluptuous, delicious lips! "You're a good kisser!" she said.

I fondled her breasts through the fabric. I slipped my hand in her corduroy pants. I felt the soft flesh and the curly hair at the tips of my fingers. "No! no! no!" she protested. She hugged and held me tight and I pulled my hand out. I put her hand in my jeans. She clung to me again and kept on kissing me and pulled her hand out.

I suggested we move to a more private place. "Well, I don't know if I want to be more private," she said.

We strolled under the trees. It had been raining earlier in the day. There were so many mosquitoes! So, we turned back. We went back to the path and continued walking uphill. We reached the top of Mont Royal. We sat on a bench. We talked for a while. The sun was going down. There was scarcely anyone around. I suggested that maybe we should go.

"That's it?" she said.

She was expecting more. Or, worse, was she accusing me of having a weak sexual drive? I understood what she wanted. She wanted me to be forceful.

"Come with me!" I said.

I led her by the hand behind the bushes, on the other side of the trees, in the outgrown, wild grass. I smoothed down the tall grass. I gestured to her to lie down. I knelt between her legs. I kissed her on the mouth and, then, I turned my attention to those burgeoning breasts. I pulled up her sweater, the only piece of upper garment she wore. I caressed and kissed her breasts. I went from nipple to mouth, from mouth to nipple with abandoned, vigorous frenzy.

She helped me unbutton my shirt. I pressed my naked chest against her supple breasts.

I worked out all kinds of positions to direct the erection in my trousers against her crotch. I wanted to pull down her trousers.

"Come on. Let's go!" I said.

"No, I can't. Are you crazy?"

I was not satisfied. My roused desire demanded more. I rolled her on top of me. She was smiling to her heart's content. I felt again her breasts against my chest. I worked my way inside her trousers and I cupped her *patanella* in my hand.

"Come on, **Debbie**, let's do it."

"No, Achille! I said no and it is no!"

"Let's try anal. There's no danger there."

"I know it's not dangerous."

"Are you sure you don't want to? Let me!"

"No, because I came here with the intention not to."

"There's no danger."

"I know, but…"

I pulled open my zipper. I thrust my penis against the fabric covering her crotch. The fabric was too rough. Of all things, she wore corduroy pants! I moved my penis up to her navel, to her stomach, and to her breasts and then, in the frenzy of the moment, enclosing it between her soft breasts.

After that, we switched position. I lay down and she was astraddle on top of me, with me poking her trousered, treasured crotch.

"Here, let me do it!" she said and took my penis in her hand. But she was rough. And I had to coach her, "Slowly! Gently. It's better not to touch the tip."

"Like this?"

It felt good, but, now, that feeling was outweighed by a stronger sensation assailing my body. I became aware of all the mosquitoes hovering around us. In the excitement I had dismissed them. But now I started to feel the sting of the mosquitos' bites. It was like being on fire all over. I didn't have to ask. I knew my poor Debbie was going through the same thing. We had to get out of there!

I pulled up my underwear and pants, discarding the weeds and all. She helped me arrange my shirt and I pulled down her sweater to protect her from the mosquitoes.

"I'm sorry!" she said, as we were getting out from behind the bushes. She meant my not reaching orgasm.

"I'm sorry too!" I said. I meant the mosquitoes bites.

We came down the mountain. We crossed the playground. We reached the road and waited for the bus by the Cartier monument.

To the bus driver, I said, "They're as big as dragonflies." I meant the mosquitoes.

Never again! No more mosquitoes! Never uncover you ass in the bushes at dusk!

ON THE BED
I remembered the night I asked her to go and make love someplace comfortable. "No mosquitoes this time. We'll go to a motel." I said. No objection! I don't know why she agreed to go to a motel with me, but I'll always be grateful.

I was waiting in the Sherbrooke Metro Station. Among the people waiting on the subway platform, in the quiet tranquility of the evening, a weekend evening, under the high, tunnel-like ceiling of the station, a thought comes forth, an uneasiness was taking me, like the night before when riding the bus and going to visit Caroline. Suppose she misunderstood me, suppose she couldn't come and couldn't call me because she didn't have my phone number, or suppose she misunderstood me and she's waiting outside the metro station. That it was for seven o'clock, this was very clear, but perhaps not. Yesterday night, when I saw her on campus, we didn't talk about our appointment. What's in for her, anyhow? She knows what's expected of her.

Such were my thoughts. I tried to put them off. It was only seven and the appointment was from seven to seven fifteen. All I had to do was wait. I stopped pacing up and down the platform and checked if one of the people waiting there was she. I couldn't see well the people waiting on the platform on the other side, but the train had stopped twice there, leaving the platform empty, except for an old lady.

I was waiting by the exit. The thought came to me again that she might be waiting outside the ticket booth, at the entrance of the station. I rode with her in the metro once, during school time, and she had to get off at Peel Station. That meant she would get off on the other side. A train had just stopped there and I was walking up the stairs to go to the other side, when I saw her at the top of the stairs. What I fool I had been for worrying like that!

"Hi!" she said.

"Hi!" I said. "Did you see me?"

"Yes, I saw you. I just got off the train."

I took both her hands in mine and kissed her on the lips and said, "Thank you!"

"What was that for?" she said.

"For being considerate, for caring, for keeping the appointment."

We took the train heading north. We did not speak much on the way to the motel. There was no problem getting our room. It was upstairs. A cleaning lady gave us directions. We made some comments about the room. She went to the bathroom. I turned on the TV.

We were hugging each other. I moved with her ever closer to the edge of the bed and I pushed her on the bed with me falling on top of her. I kissed and licked her face. As we got rid of our clothes, I kept kissing her at different stages of undress. I recall with fondness feeling her breasts, unbuttoning her trousers, and touching her crotch through the flimsy panties.

"Are using the diaphragm?" I asked.

"Yes? Come on!" And she pulled me towards her.

She kicked her panties off, opened her legs, and raised her knees.

She gave a **quiet cry**. But, for me, it was too good! It was too much! I gave a **loud cry** and I ejaculated. And it was done! The energy I had conserved during the whole week was gone. I was spent.

"We have to wait a while," I said. "You didn't come."

In the meantime, I amused my fellow writer by saying, "In Scene One, I see myself in the estate of my late father in the countryside of my native small town. From the second story bedroom where I have been masturbating, I'm looking down onto the large courtyard, where my friends are waiting for me to start the soccer game. In Scene Two, I see myself at night in that same bedroom, in the faint electric light, just before going to bed, after opening the window and breathing in the fresh evening air, I stretch and tighten my legs, one by one, to admire the beauty of their outline. And, in Scene Three, I see myself with this girl in the corn patch and I am rubbing my penis between her legs, but her underwear at her ankles is frustrating my efforts... Now it's your turn to tell me a story."

"What can I say?"

"Anything that passes through your mind. Anything will do."

"This is what comes to mind. This boyfriend of mine I had once, he always wanted me to bring my girlfriend along to pair her off with his friend. All he wanted, his friend, was sex. My girlfriend had a boyfriend, who had never touched her, because she would not let him."

I was ready to go at it again when she said, "No. Wait!" She slid down on the bed with her head at the level of my loins and stopped, resting her face on my belly.

"Shall I?" she said.

"Yes!" I said.

Ah! The feel of her mouth! Her hot tongue as it swept over the tip! Each sweep brought a new fresh, warm, shattering sensation. Each time an impulse ran down my spine and I twitched in her mouth. And, intuitively, my hands gripped her hair.

I thought, 'Lick, lick, my lover!'

This was my first blowjob. How many times had I wished for this? It was so much better than what I had imagined. O my lover Debbie!

It didn't take long. I felt an overpowering pleasure. My grip on her head lost tightness. And I began gently stroking her hair.

Later, on my way home, in the metro train, I glanced this girl she had just gotten on the train. She had her back to me but I suspected she was beautiful. She was standing in the middle of the car with this not-so-attractive girl with rouged cheeks. As the train started to move forward, she swung around the vertical pole she was hanging on and her face came to me in full view. I saw that beautiful she was indeed, as my suspicions had given me to believe. She reminded me of my lover Debbie. O untried woman!

Outside, as I waited for the Fleury bus, a man stood in front of me. His face was square, brown, and rough like that of a brick. He was balding. His skull was shrunk. And, through the unbuttoned shirt, I could see his ribs. He had the semblance of a living corpse. And the cemetery was nearby! O tried man!

The brick-faced man followed with his skeleton eyes the two large birds that flew above the tall trees of the graveyard and soared out of sight. This was the graveyard I passed by with my lover Debbie. On the way to the motel, I said, "You know, all these tombs without crosses seemed odd to me before, but now they don't." And on the way back, after we made love,

I said, "Supposing you believe in an after life, do you believe in punishment and reward up there?" "No," she said, "because who is going to tell us what's wrong?"

ON THE BRINK

Upstairs, in the library, I saw Juliana, I girl I had asked out. She gave me her phone number, but there was no service on her phone number. When I asked her about it, she said, "I have a class now." And I had to meet Debbie in the cafeteria.

When I got to the cafeteria, Debbie was already there. She was sitting with a girlfriend. I said hello to her hi. She introduced her friend. Her name was Joanne. I sat down with them. They continued their conversation. For a while, I was paying attention to Joanne, who gabbed nonstop. At one point, I went for a drink without saying anything.

On my way back, I saw Juliana with one of the two oriental guys who were with her in the library. If she saw me, she wasn't fazed; but I didn't care.

When I got back to my seat, I teased Debbie, "You wouldn't let me have some of your yogurt, but I'll let you have some of my drink."

Joanne continued talking to her. I thought, 'Doesn't she ever stop?' And finally she went away. I remained alone with Debbie.

"I couldn't come on Tuesday, I'm sorry." I said.

"I's all right," she said in nodding her head.

"You have a mark on you cheek."

"You better say that."

"What is it? A hickey?

"Oh, you!"

There was a pause of silence. Sometimes, I was conscious about making conversation with her. I asked her if I could read her short story.

"Do you want to read it? Really?" she said. She revealed her eagerness, her excitement about her writing.

It was a surrealistic story about a dummy, not a dead man.

When I was finished, she said, "Do you find it is too short?"

I liked the story and I told her.

Then, I asked her when it would be possible for us to go out again.

"No," she said. "I wanted to talk to you about that. I've thought about us and I've decided not to do that again."

"Why? If that is what you wish. Why this sudden decision? Why not before? Have you talked to somebody and been swayed?"

"No. Who was I going to tell? I don't have anyone..."

"Perhaps not in a direct way..."

"No. It's a decision a came to by myself."

I said that we would just go out like that. "We don't have to go out every time with the purpose of having sex. Making love is not the most important thing. What is important is that we are together."

"If it's not sex, what else is there, what do we go out for? To what purpose?"

"The thought crossed my mind that you're afraid of verbal communication. Is that it?"

"I can't go out."

"Excuses," I said. "You don't have a boyfriend now. So let me be your..."

"No!"

I wanted to know the real reason. "If you have something to tell me, you tell me. I'm not afraid of being hurt. Why did you in the first place go so far if you intended to retreat after all that?"

"All right? I'll tell you. Because I wanted to be sure that you really liked me. I said to myself it wasn't fair, that I had to give it a try. Because I didn't like you physically, you see?"

"And now you've decided to end everything, just like that?" I sat back and stretched in the chair. "You're insulting me now. Listen! Anybody else would just say, 'Fuck off!' But, for the sake of writing, I will try to explain myself. You shouldn't do this to me. You're hurting me. Because you want to become a writer I expect sense from you. This is going to influence me in my life. Because you said I'm no good as a man, no good physically."

"No, I didn't say that. You're twisting the meaning of my words. I just said... It's not what I'm looking for."

"You've become an idealist now? Why then?"

"I wanted to make sure... You're all right as a man."

"You used me then?"

"You men are all alike. All you want from a girl is sex."

"Don't give that 'you men'..."

"All right. I'll say... you!"

"I told you everything about myself..."

"You see? It's exactly this I'm afraid of. It's attachment I'm afraid of. It's better to stop now before complications, later it would be harder..."

I was thinking of my appointment with my lover Bree on Saturday. "Perhaps, this is the time I should say, 'Fuck off!' and leave you here."

"Shh! Marianne is coming." Marianne was another friend of hers.

"All right, but you're going to talk to me. You won't do like with the other girl, talk to her all the time."

Marianne sat at our table. Usual greetings and introductions!

"It's 6:30," I said to Debbie. "Let's go out for a moment. Leave your things here."

"Will you be here, Marianne?" she said, turning to her friend for support.

Marianne was very agreeable. We went out. We went up the wooden stairway. She seemed pleased to walk up those stairs, like the first time, what it meant.

"Let's go back to our argument," I said.

Going over the same things all over again, I tried to persuade her, "Listen! Next time, I won't think of my pleasure. I'll do all I can to let you come."

"Why would you do that?"

"Because I care. I want you to feel about me the way I feel about you."

"No. It would be futile, because I can't come."

Coming back from the walk, I said, "I want to write short stories on our experiences!"

"Really?"

"I have notes, stacks of them. I see! This makes you happy, but what about the rest..."

She looked pleased. The Greek guy we met before passed by and said hi to us.

We walked towards the same corner I brought her the first night, the night I asked her out. I walked on the tree trunk as she walked beside me. I put my arm around her and she said, "And all this led to that."

Staring to the school entrance, I said, "What I'm looking for in life is… enlightenment. The way I want to attain it is through… writing." Then, turning to her, I added, "Will you be my partner in crime?"

She lowered her head. She stayed like that for a while. I was concerned. Then, she looked up.

"I thought you were crying and, instead, you're smiling. It's a big joke to you, eh?"

"You take me for being good," she said.

"It's useless trying to convince you, if you have already made up your mind," I said.

"Who knows? Tomorrow, I might change my mind," she said.

I was leaving. "Go in peace!" I said.

"You'll find the right girl," she said.

"I already did. She's standing in front of me."

She stopped there, not going and staring into my eyes. "Why don't you go now?" I said. "You say you don't want see me and you're still here?" But these were words being spoken to some other girl. She was still standing there. I bent over and whispered into her ear, "Our lovemaking is not over!"

8B. My Lover Bree

OBSESSION
I am much saturated
with my love for you;
and you give me no outlet.
I am dangerous to you now;
I could burst with my love.
I feel my heart gripped,
held by a painful grasp.
Those are your latches
locking the gates to my heart
that wants to flood out,
erupt like a volcano,
and submerge you with love.

BREE, IN COLLEGE

My story with my lover **Bree** (short for Briseis) starts **in college**. It was **a fine April day**. I met Tricia, the Trinidadian girl, at John Gabot's Square, at the bus stop. She was nice and lively. As I was talking to Tricia, I noticed my lover Debbie was at the end of the bus queue. In the bus, I should've sat with Debbie; but, against my better judgment, I sat with Tricia. I blame my Christian altruism for that. Debbie, sitting in front of us, got mad at me. She got off at Selby without saying goodbye.

Engrossed in our conversation, Tricia and I got off one stop after the Richelieu one. I promised her I would ask my friend Fanny to help her with her psychology questions. Mr. D, the Poetry teacher, called me from across the street to tell me, "I don't know when your 'thing' is going to take place." By 'thing' he meant my presentation. Teachers were protesting reclassification. I gave Tricia an appointment in the study room for 2:20 to introduce her to my friend Fanny.

There was no one in the Religion classroom. And, since my friend Fanny was not there, I went to give a look in the study room, to see if Tricia was there. Past the study room, I met Bob from the Philosophy class. He was just coming up with a friend of his. He said, "I've been thinking about what you've been saying. It's becoming clearer." I told him what Barbara had said and started talking about my new enlightenment, **world conception** through magnetic, ideographic, a tabular systems; but he had to go to class. Anyway, he was interested in what I was trying to explain and that was good.

On going back to the Religion classroom, my future lover Bree was coming up behind me. "Hi, enemy!"

"Enemy?"

"You were attacking me yesterday, in the Philosophy class."

"No, it wasn't me. It was Bob and What's-her-name (the blond, long-haired girl) and May too."

"Yes, even her, even her."

"But, Achille, I want to know what Sartre says!"

"I realize that. I am sorry I used up the time with my position."

At first, when we went inside the Religion room, she sat down and I went to the window to look outside. She got up and I turned towards her. She came towards me and looked at me full in the face, as we came at no more than a foot and a half from each other. Ah, to view her in all her splendor that close! She wanted to ask about the example of the bull and the bullfighter.

"I wanted to show, demonstrate what it is that makes man," I said.

The teacher, Mr. J, came in. We went to sit down. We were talking all excitedly about the will, Sartre, and what had happened in the philosophy class when Bree wanted me to tell the teacher about what was happening. I didn't want to. I knew it would prove useless, anyway. But the teacher wanted to 'preach' about the teachers' declassification and the signature sheet first. After that, we went to his office with the bearded guy and the girl complaining about her bastard ex-boyfriend.

(The teacher had been helping himself of Bree's cigarettes and was smoking.)

We talked about suicide and about everything and nothing: psychology, French, Jung, etc. The teacher was citing books here, authors there, and not a single thought of his own. I didn't want to assert my views; otherwise, as it happened in the philosophy class, I was going to be hated for it.

I was watching Bree. Oh, if she would turn and smile towards me! To make her laugh with me! "Bree!" I wanted to shout, to make her look at me.

The teacher was friendlier with the two girls than with us guys. First, the bearded guy and the ex-boyfriend girl left. Then, the teacher, Bree and I left. I had to go and see Tricia in the study room. Bree told me again that she wasn't opposing me in the philosophy class. I was going up the stairs and Bree and the teacher were going down. Tricia was not there. It was a little past 2:30.

On coming out of the building, I saw that Bree was there, like a jewel, outside the exit doors. "There you are!" I said, as I was opening the door. Mr. J was at her feet, sitting on the steps. She said to wait. We would be going together to Selby. The teacher was coming too, but he had to go and move his car. As he did that, I put to practice what I had just been thinking about.

"About you opposing me, if I said it, it was because I cared, because it is you, because I like you, Bree."

"Oh, thank you, Achille!" And didn't she go off balance! She swayed with her body, as if pushed, tossed backwards.

"Don't blush now!" I said,

And she laughed and laughed, so heartedly. My Bree laughed with me! Did she care about me? Did she blush because of me?

The teacher came back. "Let's go!" he said. I was walking at her right. But, as we had just passed the bus stop, Herr H, the German teacher, who was picketing, called me. I said, "See you! Bye!"

I was very blunt with Herr H., like I had never been before, "Why did you do that? I was being carried away by that girl!" I said.

Bree, I vibrate in your presence,
Because I am the string
That your hand plucks.

Bree, I vibrate in your presence,
Because I am a love instrument.

Ah, if you would vibrate for me!

Friday, May 5, there was no Religion class. In the Richelieu building, I was at the top of the staircase. Annemarie called, "Come down! Bree and I want to talk to you. We are going for a coffee at the restaurant." At the restaurant the Italian girl joined us. Bree left for her physical. I was at a loss when she said she was going skydiving on the weekend. *She is high class, chic, always nice, speckless. She has the confidence that beauty and wealth give rise to.*

I went with Annemarie afterwards. First we went to the Selby caf. Then, we went for a walk on St. Catherine. Bree ran up to us when we were just talking about her. Then she went her way. I went with Annemarie to the Air Canada Building. I met Ian there. "I finally got published!" he said.

Friday, May 11, I met Mauro at the Selby caf. After my Poetry exam, I went with him to the Canadian Armed Forces. He was thinking about enrolling.

Friday, May 18, I daydreamed about Bree. I sing like a bird for her. She comes to visit me after a long time. Welcome! I love you, Bree!

Back to reality, I brought my philosophy paper to Mrs. D's office.

BREE, IN UNIVERSITY
My story with my lover Bree continues **three years later**, in March. Bree and I were both **going to Concordia University**.

I got back home after my night with Bree. After I took a shower, looking into the backyard from the kitchen, I realized the dreariness and emptiness of my place, as compared to her downtown life. Bree is right! While I live a life, she lives a thousand more. What am I doing here? I should wake up. I should stop daydreaming!

I'll forever be haunted by images of you, Bree! These are the main memories I have from last night.

(1) I remember your liveliness from the first moment I was with you in the caf at the Norris Building, to walking on St. Catherine, Bleury, and other streets, and to waiting in line to get to see Fellini's *Amarcord*. How can anyone compare to you?

(2) I remember your loveliness, when I saw you naked. How could anyone match the way you look?

(3) I remember your sweetness, like when, with the touch of your hand on my forehead, you woke me up this morning. How can anyone match your smile, you lips?

But, why are our values so divergent? Why is it that what I want is so different from what you want? For me you are the one. For you I am just one more lover.

Even so, do I want a world without Bree? No! Never!

Help me understand you, Bree. Help me! I feel so much drawn to you. I want to be with you all the time. I feel so miserable without you. Is it possible for you to help me? Could you let me feel as you feel? Could you? So I would not be in such pain?

All things considered, what I got from you yesterday night, making love to you, is the greatest thing that could've happened to me in my life. O Bree!

It's time I start restructuring my thinking about my feelings, i.e. the way Bree makes me feel and the way I make my future lover Rosalinda feel, like when I told her we would go out. Compromise! Compromise! Will I ever be able to say, "I'm satisfied with you!"

Not to forget Rosalinda! She got attached to me in the same way I got attached to Bree.

As to Bree, the one thing I could not accept of her is when she decided to take part in the porno film made by the senior Cinema students. This has turned me off. It is too much against my values. She was supposed to be in a lesbian scene. But, what I want the most is to make love to her again and again and again.

Yesterday night I called Bree from the phone in the Norris building lobby. I was crying as I was talking to her. I never cried so much in my life. I was telling her how much I loved her after having called her "fucken bitch!" which amused her and it seemed that she liked my selfish demands to possess her.

She said, "I guess it is what everybody is looking for, unconditional love, to be loved above anything else."

I certainly don't want to amuse you. I do want to give you ecstasy, yes, but not amuse you. When we finally ended our phone conversation I said to her, "I love you, Bree!"

"You are mistaken, Achille!" she said.

I cannot understand those values: "Love is love and remains love, and then there is eating and drinking" as to her saying that lovemaking for her is like eating. But how can one greatly appreciate something if one does not greatly value that something? The greater the desire, the greater the pleasure, isn't it? Love is a great want, not a small one. It cannot be like the simple desire for eating and drinking.

I imagined of asking her, next time I talked to her, "How many lovers have you had since the last time I saw you?"

BREE, IN HEAVEN
A year later, it was a Saturday and I spent it with my lover Bree. This was the most wonderful day in my

life. Unfortunately, it was also followed by the most awful day of my life.

All of Friday night, after the phone call with her, I kept smiling and telling myself, "Hey, I've got a date with Bree!" And I thought of telling her that to amuse her.

We met in the Hall Building lobby at 2:10 in the afternoon. We went to see *Network* at the Claremont Theatre; after the movie, we went to Dunn's for a smoked meat sandwich; after that, we played two machines at the Penny Arcade's; and then we went to her one-room apartment.

She showed me her plants, her family pictures, when she was small and younger, Dawson and the longer curly hair; I particularly liked a picture of when she was sixteen or eighteen, in miniskirt, the longer curly hair, and standing by a car with her uncle; slides from John-Michael's porno film that Jay took, ... and some Amaretto we drank.

If she had told me, I would have left at that point. But then it happened that she was stretching her upper body on the bed; there, in front of me, she was inviting me; and I said, "Can I kiss you?" I said that twice. And she reached with her arm to make me go towards her... mellow and beautiful Bree, all for me... and she was kissing me.

And I had Bree in the most beautiful way that I could've ever daydreamed of. When I took off my hat, she said, "That's better, that's much better." She wanted to come first. As I was having the time of my life with one of her small, sexy breasts, she said, "The way you suck is beautiful. I like the way you suck, you know!" Ah! to feel her come, clutch my fingers, and wail with pleasure! Just before she had said, "Suck! Suck!" And earlier than that, "I want you to feel me come."

And then it was my turn. And I prayed to God to guide me. And I said, "Bree! Bree!" when it was my turn to wail. (Later, she talked of this moment, this instant, as a moment of unison, of meeting, of sharing, of being one.) And never I kissed with her more passionately as right after I climaxed. (I can understand now why Debbie and Rosalinda kissed me passionately after they made me climax.)

And then I helped her (and myself) again by sucking on her other breast.

"Imagine what this does for my self-confidence. It's fantastic!" I told her.

"I'm glad to help," she said.

"I'm going to sleep well tonight," I said.

"Good!" she said.

But after my first sleep, I woke up and stayed awake for quite a long time. I looked at the window, the jungle of plants, 'the parent, the child, and the grandchild', the way she called them. I thought if there would be a Peeping Tom in the facing building and getting the view of love making in a jungle scene. I thought of the beauty of having her there, next to me. I was listening to her breathing, but then I focused to the strange, heavy-with-menace sounds coming from outside the building into the building. They were slowly coming up the front entrance stairs and approaching ever closer along the corridor. Now, I could tell it was the heavy footsteps of a guy wearing winter boots. He stopped right outside Bree's apartment! He knocked three times on her door, as a signal. I froze. She did not hear and did not move. There was a long pause. Three more knocks on the door followed, clearer than before. She woke up and looked at me. I looked puzzled (I guess). She went and crouched at the door keyhole, her naked back and bottom to me.

"Who is it?" she said.

The guy answered.

"John? I thought you were gone." For a moment I feared she would let him in. "John, I am not alone!"

"Okay. I'll call you tomorrow. Bye!"

"Bye!" She got back in bed. The guy was walking away.

I felt so much alienated and hurt. I wished for the guy's death. He had disturbed my happiness. He had destroyed the slight hope that I might become Bree's lover. But this was her reality. How could I suddenly barge into her life and expect... What she had done for me, what she had meant to me... She was awake... by the way she moved. I got close to her and put my arm around her. She placed my hand on her breasts. Later, she said she was hot, I took my arm away, and she said, "Thank you, Achille!"

I went to sleep again and woke up at 9:00. I wanted to make out, but she said she wanted to sleep some more. I went to the washroom. And nothing happened later. The daylight of the morning had destroyed all romanticism that there might have been early on.

She made light tea with honey, read the paper on the carpet. I dressed. She said she was going to wait for John's call. She said she was worried about him. "Something was wrong otherwise he would not have come at four o'clock in the morning," she said. She also said he was a musician and he was supposed to be in the Laurentians and... he was her lover.

A next time! Who knows? I mentioned again doing my photo project with her. I twice kissed her and wetted her lower lip. She didn't kiss back. And then I forgot my gloves.

About me, she said...

"You know, I'm jealous of your skin. It's so smooth." (She was caressing me from my belly to my chest, when she said that.)

"Why should you be fatter?" (About my trying to become fatter.)

"Bald is distinguishing… Depending on the face. You have a nice face. You look good bald." (We were crossing Sherbrooke to get to the bus stop in front of the Museum of Fine Arts.) And, when I took off my cap, "That's better. That's much better."

"I'm looking at your profile. You have a beautiful nose." (When we were in bed.)

What does all this mean for me? She made me feel good about my looks. What more dare I ask? This was Bree, the Bree of my dreams, since the Dawson days. Thank you, Bree! To simply talk to you is a privilege.

Never my face looked more beautiful as that Sunday morning at my home after I took a shower, my lips softened by Bree's kisses.

Her response to me (her kissing me, her caressing me) has taken such a long time. The first time was in 1973, when we were in the same Philosophy class at Dawson College. How desired you were, Bree! From those Dawson days to today! As if this was due to me.

That she's mine or not, I can't imagine my world without Bree in it. She's perfect. She's the epitome of the fair sex.

You are like sunshine. As such, I can't have you just to myself. You belong to everybody.

BREE, IN THE FAMILY WAY

Two years later, I met her on the Sherbrooke bus. I greeted her and gave her my seat. She was pregnant and she talked about eating healthy. She was getting married soon. Yet, once she'd told me, "You don't want to relate to only one view of the world, which would happen if you were to marry to one person."

8C. My Lover Monique

I was going to university at the time. It was summertime. We met in an art education class. We hit it off right away. It was instant attraction. We shared the same passion for drawing. And, during class, we would communicate via goofy cartoon drawings, her specialty.

Our relationship was idyllic. We made love and worked together on our education projects.

Monique had no family in Montreal. I took her home to meet my family. She was very excited. She stayed the night. She was the first woman I made love with in my own bed.

Then, things turned sour and, to this day, I don't know why. She didn't want to make love anymore. And the final straw came when I found out that, behind my back, she was planning to have sex with her neighbour. And that was it! I could no longer trust her.

After our relationship failed, I wrote a poem to express salient moments and feelings I'd had with her.

FREE BIRD

When did you go swimming, Monique?
Why does it matter when?
You're not supposed to do that.
I want to do what I like.

Freedom is to fulfil your love.
But the lover has no freedom.

I'll return what you gave me.
You don't need to. I have your ring.
It's a gift for the gift you gave me.
Have I given you a gift?
Yes. You loved me once.

That day, the first day, we were at the amusement park.
Aujourd'hui je suis tombe amoureuse d'un Canadien, you said.
And then sitting in the semi-darkness and licking ice cream
You're eyes shine! you said
And yours too, I said.
It's because of the lights, you said
It's because of the moon, I said.
Next day, fresh from a bath, ever so softly,
You let me make love to you, my love.
The greatest gift that one can give another

Since that day my love for you has been growing,
But yours has been diminishing.
One morning you wanted me to go to the pharmacy.
But the pharmacy was closed.
I could get what we needed but I waited for you,
To make it the natural way you wanted.
One night you promised, "In the morning!"
And then in the morning you said, "I can't!"
And more excuses:
You would not let me make love to you even though you could.
And more nonsense:
About the spiritual way you have to feel in order to make love.
I felt cheated, deceived in my love.
To make love, that was what was lacking to make it complete.
I even believed that you wanted me to be rough in order to give.
I was remembering your story of the Norwegian guy.
You said he was rough and next day you could not walk.
And, since you seemed to have liked it that way,
I tried; I tried again, and harder this time.

I hurt you and the harsh words, Take it out!
But I love you! I love you!
I was wrong in my belief. I felt ashamed.
You made me think that you liked it rough,
But there is no excuse for that.
I am possessive, but never violent.

I want you to be my friend, **only**, you said.
Never to make love again!
At least before I was waiting for the right time.
Could I limit myself to Platonic love?
What some friends of mine have?
Sex is very important to me.
I can't imagine a world without it.

But that is not all:
The way you kissed and now kiss:
The way you let me kiss you.
You tortured me with your tongue.
Now, you seldom kiss the way you used to.
Oh, ecstasy! Your tongue in my mouth!
Once I caught your laughter in my mouth!

It is your fault. I blame you for this.
A bad feeling sprouts when a wish is unfulfilled.
It halted the growth of our relationship,
Like an unripe apple that begins to rot.

That was a life lived in dreams.
That is a ghost I cannot fight.
As if spirituality in lovemaking were not enough,
You want idealism lived in reality?

You, free bird,
Come and touch
And then depart in flight,

Like the darting kisses of that first night
You would then laugh
And then go back to your dreams.

You, free bird,
You come along,
Ever so attractive,
And, ever so sweetly, touch,
And then you depart in flight.
You touch
But you never give.
You love,
But you never make love.

People love you,
And you love people.
Everybody is your friend,
None is your lover.
You belong to all
And yet you belong to none.

If this is your attitude,
To treat people like you treat me,
What am I to be jealous of?

Depart in flight, free bird!
Your game is the right one.
One can't ever have you.
You take; you never give
You'll be forever ephemeral.

You can't ever return my gift.
My gift is the gift of love, my love for you.

9A. My Intended Rosalinda

IN THE END
When I'll be old and lonely
and the painful remembrance
that you were not to be mine
will be the comforting companion
of my quieter setting heart,
I'll recall that, in my life, at one time
you were the splendor of great beauty.
I wake up and rise the fallowing morning
in the high valleys of a golden dawn,
and I'll see you as one more light glowing
and you'll be smiling and knowing
I was in love with you, Rosalinda.

Maurizio was my friend. We had met in the summer of 1968, when I was pursuing Louise. **Rosalinda** was Maurizio's sister-in-law. She was crazy about me, and Maurizio's wife and her parents approved of us being an item. At the beginning, I would visit Maurizio to see her. Then, I would go and visit her directly. They lived in a duplex. Maurizio and his wife lived upstairs and she and her parents lived downstairs.

FIRST TIME
I was going to university at the time. She was in her last year of college. I was alone with her in her bedroom. I was supposed to help her study. She took off the elastic holding her hair. How much more beautiful she looked with her hair cascading on the side of her face! The paleness of her flesh contrasted with the blackness of her hair. Her closeness made

me sneeze. I was getting aroused. Standing in front of the dresser mirror she showed me that her mother had cut her hair in front.

I got her elastic and wouldn't give to her. "I want you like that," I said.

She sat on the bed. I was kneeling in front of her, worshipping my beautiful girlfriend. "Do you think I am beautiful like that?" she said.

"No! You're ugly," I said. But what I meant was exactly the opposiste. I got aroused. I lay on top of her on the bed with my swollen crotch touching hers. Oh, her warm body! The heat of her body warming me up!

We were wrestling for the possession of her hair elastic. I touched her thighs, buttocks, and crotch, when she banged on my nose with her fist! Then, pretending to bite her, I tried to kiss her rosy, soft, beautiful cheek. But, she avoided my kiss and, in the process, she got a little scratch under her ear. Consoling her as she sat on the bed, kneeling, so helpless, but smiling. O beautiful girl of mine!

SECOND TIME

I was sitting at her desk, in her bedroom. She wanted to write. She sat on my thigh as she wrote. O her warm heavenly embrace of my thigh! So beautiful! So lovely! Knowing that her beautiful *patanella* was pushing on my thigh! Clutching her leg between my legs with my other leg to hold her tighter. Leaning forward against her back to bring her closeer to my chest, my heart. I was so close to her cheek with my mouth! I was about to pull up her sweater and she said, "What are you doing?" I would have continued anyway, but she wore a bra. Asked her why she wore a bra.

And, throughout all this, her parents were in the kitchen. We heard her father coming to tell us that it was time to eat. I lowered my knee and she stood up all the while continuing with her writing. During supper she played footsy with me under the table. I love you, beautiful! I felt such genuine love for her.

Later, in her room, she was hugging me tight. I had to break it for fear that one of her parents might come. Still later, she showed her letter to me: "Dear Mr. Achille, you have a nice, beautiful girlfriend. Sincerely, Miss Rosalinda."

Outside, on my way home, I was thinking that she was the one for me. I was thinking of the day I would be asking her to marry me, and all the nice things I'd give her.

THIRD TIME

I still felt her lock of love on my upper thighs. And I had the smell of her sweat in my nostrils. I wanted to lie on the bed. I wanted to be still. I wanted to savour what had passed, the lock of her thighs around my thighs. I didn't want to do anything but savour the bliss that that lock of love had given me.

The way she rubbed on me! For a moment I thought I brought her to the same bliss she'd given me. Rubbing on me, harder and harder, my hands on her buttocks, she moaned as if she was in pain. I had just come but I continued my rubbing for her. As she grew more frantic, her cheek on my breast (I found later that my shirt was wet with her saliva), she subsided with her rhythmic movements and then dismounted from me and went away. She said she wanted to get a drink of water in the kitchen.

After we went downstairs to clean the walkway covered with snow, she lay on the bed with me, facing in the opposite direction. After some initial protests, she welcomed my rubbing her crotch with my foot. She made it into a game. "I'll push your leg and you push mine," she said and she began the rhythmic movement of her body against my foot. And then she, 'inadvertently', took my hand and put it on her crotch. And I obliged to her pleasure.

She was all over me. "Lift me up!" she said different times. We played "spin-the-bottle". And, I finally kissed her... twice. I finally kissed those lips of hers I'd dreamed of kissing for so long. It was her 'penalty' for losing. Then, on the bed, she would jump on top of me. At one time, I was on top of her. But, she said, "I am suffocating. I want to be on top." And, it was all that that led to our rubbing each other on the bed.

We were wrestling on the bed when I did it. I slipped my hand in her pants under the pantyhose. I finally touched that crotch I had so many times stroked and cupped from outside her pants. There was a little bit of hair as I imagined it to be. And I held her *patanella* in my hand, pressing down with my middle finger.

"Achille! What are you doing?" she cried.

Then, she got up, turned off the light, and came to lie on the bed with me. She lay with me in the dark, but she would not kiss me.

"That's all. That's how far I go," she said and smacked a kiss on my cheek. I wanted to kiss her on the mouth, but she hugged me tight to prevent me from kissing her. She liked to be snug with me on the bed and in the dark.

I made her come on top of me to have her repeat the memory of that lock of love. And she began the morose stirring, rubbing on my crotch.

"I don't want," she said at first, but then she yieldied. Was it my stroking of her buttocks that changed her mind?

Once, I tried to put my hand in her pants between her buttocks, but she protested, "Oh, Achille!"

And then her moaning subsided with her stirring. She was fast. And she wanted to go to the kitchen.

"But I am not finished!" I told her. "I need more time!"

She turned on the light and left me like that. I guess it was a good thing because her parents came home right after.

FORTH TIME

I was locked in a hug, with her on top of me, on the couch. I heard her parents coming up the stairs and opening the door of the apartment. I was under her. I could not move. She was feverish. I had to tap her hard on her back to get her attention, to make her aware of what was happening.

I broke away from her. She got up and rushed to meet her parents. I stood up, trying to find myself. I was at a loss. What to do? I pushed my hair in place, combing it slowly with my fingers as though my central nervous system was going through a malfunction. It took me sometime before I regained control of myself. I was lucky that she distracted her parents and her father didn't come into the living room till much later.

FIFTH TIME

Once, we pretended to go out to the movies and instead we went to Brian's apartment. He left when we got there. I had arranged that with him. We were there alone and she got all naked for me to make me explore her virgin body. Of course, my focus was her crotch. I bent down and kissed those soft thighs and especially her beautiful *patanella*. She gave me a hand job and, at the end of it, she kissed me ever so passionately. But, I didn't make love to her! Was it that strange apartment? Was it my Christian altruism? Or, was it because I loved her? Whatever it was, it was the wise thing to do, because I didn't end up marrying her after all. And that is something I have regretted for the rest of my life!

9B. My Intended Ginette

NECESSARY TURMOIL

There must always be
This turmoil in me
If I don't want to see
The end of my identity.
For I know it would
If this cease should.

I know I must continue my quest
With each tomorrow be at unrest
Forever I must hope and strive
And be stronger and survive
Whatever the failure will be
That each tomorrow will bring me.

Ginette was a French teacher at the high school where I worked. **It was my first year of teaching.**

I would see her from time to time at staff meetings. One day, I was alone with her in the library, I got the courage, and I asked her out. She agreed and gave me her phone number.

It was wintertime, the first night we went out. When we got to her apartment, I warmed her feet against my belly, and we made love. "It was a mistake to make love the first time we went out," she later complained.

Anyway, after that first time, it became a habit to leave work together, get some food, and make love.

I discovered some peculiarities about her I wished she did not have. She wanted to sleep with the window open in the middle of winter. Her lovemaking was limited to the missionary position. And she was a groupie to this psychologist/guru who spewed out common sense.

There was something else. She told me about this handsome guy who had lived with her to show that he could be with an unattractive girl. Why had she put up with rubbish like that?

I brought her home to meet my family. My mother told me that my younger brother had said, "Achille took his time but he found himself some pretty girl."

We celebrated Christmas at my house and New Year's Eve at her parents' house, located outside the city. I brought her retired father a bottle of cognac. He was very happy. I ate tourtière (meat pie), a traditional Québecois dish, for the first time.

Another time, we went up north to shovel snow off the roof of her older sister's house. I nearly fell off the roof because I was wearing these boots with used soles. Afterwards, I remember having this animated discussion in English with her younger brother's Italian girlfriend.

Some things happened that undermined my love for her.

During the summer break, instead of spending the time with me, she chose to go, for two weeks, to the guru's retreat outside the city. I spent the time making the staircase railing for my newly-built house.

She brought me to see the guru at his office. The whole thing took the guise of an intervention. He suggested that I transform my bungalow into a duplex, so we could have our own apartment. He knew a lot about municipal zoning laws! She told me, later, that she had to pay him for that rubbish.

There was an after-work party at our school. I didn't want to go but she went anyways. And what was worse, she flirted and danced with this teacher who was a vowed adversary of mine.

The final straw happened during the winter break. I was sick with a cold for the whole week. On Monday morning, she called me. I railed at her. "For a whole week, I was sick and you didn't call me," I said, "and now you want me to give you a lift to work?" And that was it about us!

It was a good thing our relationship ended. Her behavior showed that she was not committed to us.

9C. My Intended Vita

CONSTANT YOU

In every action of yours,
you are always sweet to me.

You love me; you touch me,
you are always sweet to me.

Even when I do things you don't like,
you are still sweet to me.

Like mine, **Vita**'s family was from Sepino. Her parents were my older brother's godparents. And, her older sister was married to one of my cousins.

In Sepino, when we were children, we used to play together occasionally. In Montreal, when she came to visit my father in the hospital, I took notice of her for the first time. Years later, she came to visit my mother with her younger brother. **By this time I was working.** It was the beginning of summer and I was poised to go on vacation to Italy for the first time.

After I came back, in late fall, I called her and asked her out. She agreed! We went to see a comedy. At the theatre, we were sitting in the back. We were laughing so loudly, even at mundane situations, that people turned around to look at us.

Then, we would go out so we could make out in the car. Once, parked in front of this factory, we were so engaged when a car parked behind us. They directed their high beams at us. I was so pissed! I moved from the back seat to the driver's seat and started my car. I wanted to catch up with them but they'd driven off all too quickly.

I remember another time being in my room and reading to her an erotic story from a men's magazine.

I didn't work too far from her house. Once, she invited me for lunch during my lunch break. Her father came from work too to join us.

Another time, we went with her younger sister to see this *paroliere* (lyricist) downtown. I wasn't for the encore. It showed I wasn't interested. On the way home, I had an argument with her contrarian sister about some women's issue. Vita sided with her sister!

Yet another time, I wasn't happy about a joke her younger brother had made. I didn't say anything about it, but it showed that I was upset. Vita, then, came to my house to smooth things out. We sat at the foot of the bed in my bedroom and she would not let my touch her until she was assured of my affection for her.

I took my mother to her house. They received us with a lot of grace. That week was my birthday. I was given a beautiful sweater as a present. And they gave my mother a present too!

During the summer, my older brother was visiting from Belgium. At a get-together, one night, at my house, she got along marvelously with both my sister-in-laws. Vita was very engaging with people. And, of the three of them, she was the prettiest. She had a lovely, symmetrical face with a perfect, straight nose. After I had taken her home, my older brother said to me, "She's the one!"

One night, at her house, my cousins came over. They took with them their godfather, who played the accordion, to serenade us. Vita's parents were very surprised. These cousins of mine were the parents-in-law of their oldest daughter. They used to be very good friends. But, from the time Vita's father had built himself a huge house near the river, they had never visited. "They came because of Achille," her father said.

I proposed to her. And we decided to marry. Our favorite wedding hall was available in October.

Ode To My Fair Sex

For you were first, Annina,
For you were second, Diana,
For you were third, Anna,
I remember you, **my yearnings!**

For you gave me self-esteem, Fioretta,
for you came to my house, Lucrezia,
For you were dear to me, Ginevra,
I remember you, **my infatuations!**

For you liked me, Loredana
For you called my name, Angela
For you showed promise, Sofia
I remember you, **my prospects!**

For you were my contemplated ones, Concetta,
Patrizia, Marianne, Jeanne, Stella
For you were my doomed dates, Francine, Maureen,
Liane, Dominique
For you were my romantic pursuits, Bianca, Louise,
Amalia, Anita
I remember you, **my high school girls!**

For you were so adorable to me, Jenny
For you were my confidant, Fanny
For you were my inducements, Elena, Vicky
I remember you, **my friends!**

For you gave me so much, Debbie
For you were the finest there is, Bree
For you were my greatest regret, Monique
I remember you, **my lovers!**

For you were love at first sight, Rosalinda
For you were my long-lasting girlfriend, Ginette
You were a gift to my life, Vita
I could not forget you, **my intended!**